"In Lisa Mannetti's magical *The Box Jumper*, readers are treated to intriguing premises and finely wrought characterizations rooted in the hazy past of a bygone America. As usual, Mannetti's driving narrative propels this fascinating portrait of illusionist Harry Houdini and the strange goings on in and around—even beyond—his world. Highly recommended to all who love a great story, excellent writing, and memorable characters with a haunting literary flair."
— Jason V. Brock, author of Milton's Children and Disorders of Magnitude

"'Magic' is the operative word for this moody novella. The magic of Harry Houdini serves as an overriding backdrop here, but another kind of magic permeates these pages—the magic of fine writing. Don't expect the usual linear plot, because there is no direct narrative. Vivid dreams, surreal images, hypnotic memories, all serve to flesh out an unsettling tale that sweeps us into a new fictional dimension. Read *The Box Jumper* and share the magic."
— William F. Nolan, author of *Logan's Run* and screenwriter of *Burnt Offerings*

"Like most writers, I was fascinated by the daring exploits of the great escape artist, Harry Houdini. And I loved the clever solutions of Arthur Conan Doyle's great detective, Sherlock Homes. What a pleasure to find them both again in this story told in first person by Leona, a woman who knew and loved Harry Houdini. Lisa Mannetti cleverly interlaces fact and fiction in this exciting and sad tale. I read it through in one sitting, unable to set it down."
— Gene O'Neill, Bram Stoker Award-winning author of *The Confessions of St. Zach* and *Deathflash*

"Lisa Mannetti's *The Box Jumper* is a passionately told story of love, memory, and how we can be possessed by both. Mannetti is, simply put, a master of the dark historical fantasy, and in *The Box Jumper* she has all her talents on full display. The only really frustrating thing about her stories is how she manages to make perfection look so easy."

— Joe McKinney, Bram Stoker Award-winning author of *Dog Days* and *Plague of the Undead*

"Lisa Mannetti has given us a look into the life of a fascinating historical character and cultural icon. Her novella brims over with dark suspense and a brilliant re-creation of a New York long gone. As always, she writes with passion and originality. A great story."
— Tom Monteleone, Bram Stoker and Locus Award-winning author of *Night of Broken Souls* and *Eyes of the Virgin*

"A haunting tale of madness and mystery. Mannetti leads the reader through a thrilling maze of illusion and scandal surrounding world-famous magician and psychic debunker, Harry Houdini. As elusive as a magic trick, the story unfolds through the dubious memories of one of his former assistants who suffers from various illnesses throughout the story. Mannetti's words entice the reader to explore a lewd world of liars and lust. As the layers of intrigue unfold, the reader is compelled to keep reading and isn't disappointed."
— Sèphera Girón, author of *Flesh Failure* and *Captured Souls*

"With *The Box Jumper*, Mannetti has lovingly woven a wonderfully enigmatic spell, whisking readers away to the secret world of the great Harry Houdini and his sharp-as-a-tack assistant, Leona. Ms. Mannetti is my favorite literary conjurer."
— Charles Colyott, author of the Randall Lee Mysteries

"*The Box Jumper* is pure magic! Lisa Mannetti conjures up a story like Houdini conjured handcuffs and then returns us to reality with a bang."
— Damon Reinbold, past President of the International Brotherhood of Magicians Ring 29, Little Rock, AR, and Ring 90, Albuquerque, NM; also past President of the Society of American Magicians Assembly 71, Albuquerque, NM

"Lisa Mannetti's blend of meticulous research and melodic prose brings gut-wrenching reality to BOX JUMPER, a tale of deceit, madness, and murder. As believable as it is incredible, Mannetti's historical fiction will leave you breathless and wanting more."
— Patrick Freivald, Bram Stoker Award-nominated author of *Blood List* and *Jade Sky*.

THE BOX JUMPER

A novella by
Lisa Mannetti

Smart Rhino Publications
www.smartrhino.com

First Edition

DEDICATION

For my brother, Peter Mannetti, who, with his sharp mind, keen wit, and playful acrobatics, taught me to fly imaginatively, and most important, inspired me—much like Houdini himself—from the time of our childhood on.

THE BOX JUMPER

CONTENTS

"Box Jumper, a nickname ascribed to a magician's assistant, typically a beautiful female, and historically an icon of glamour whose principal function on stage frequently involved—among other classic roles such as handling props, levitating or vanishing—misdirecting the audience."
— *The Magician's Encyclopedia*

"The question of whether or not Houdini was deliberately killed may never be fully resolved. There is no doubt that the death of the world's greatest magician benefited the Spiritualist movement and only their movement."
— *The Secret Life of Houdini*

"Nothing may occur in a given haunted location while you're actually there—the entities affect you whenever they want to affect you—when you are at your weakest and most vulnerable."
— Lorraine Warren, co-founder of the New England Society of Psychic Research

INVITATION

It was the children who brought Houdini back. The ones who were dead or missing. He never had any of his own, but he loved children—made sure there were always free performances at hospitals and orphanages. Once, in Edinburgh, he saw so many kids running barefoot through the streets, he even bought 300 pairs of shoes for them and fitted them up at his benefit show at the Lyceum. That's the kind of man he was. He was magical all right—so much so, I think I loved him before I ever met him—back when I was just a kid myself.

He was always in the headlines. But the day I'm thinking of—when I first fell in love with him—was bitterly cold here, one day past the ides of March, not even the barest hint of spring in the air. Houdini had just become the first aviator in Australia. My father, like half the men in America and Europe, was fascinated by flying. But Harry wasn't content to read about aeronautics or merely watch newsreels. He bought a Voisin and hired a mechanic and an instructor, essentially taught himself in a matter of weeks, then took to the skies. I can still hear my father gushing over the morning newspaper, "Imagine that. Here's the guy—world famous—the king of handcuffs, the greatest escape artist of all time, and he just plunks down some money, gets him a biplane and zoom! He's airborne. It's unbelievable. What a man!" He smacked the newspaper with the back of his hand for emphasis, folded over the page so I could read it. I could hear the wind gusting outside through the thin panes of glass in the kitchen windows, smelled snow on the air. I kept thinking about swirling updrafts and crosscurrents on the trackless field near Melbourne.

Then my father, slightly chagrined, finished lacing his heavy boots, stood to down the last of the cheap coffee-milk that was his breakfast, swiped at his dripping mustache with a frazzled sleeve, and shouted he was late for work at the factory.

Still, I never forgot that note of joy and exaltation in his voice, the brilliant gleam in his eyes. For one brief moment, he was a boy again, a boy who still had dreams of flight and freedom. I knew he'd never be rich or famous, but I was glad he wasn't bitter, glad he could find a tiny sparkling bit of magic by reading about his hero. My hero, from then on, too.

I'd been born with the turn of the century. Back in those days, those of us who led narrow, trapped lives often filled the hollows created by the grind of poverty with imagination, with care-wrought scrapbooks and news clippings, glimpses of other more colorful worlds on painted posters and lithographs. I dreamed about traveling magic shows, spangled girls, and top-hatted men who wore black capes and vanished amid purple vapors and gouts of yellow flame. Dreamt about conjurors' mysteries 'til, wandering one day past Martinka's on Sixth Avenue, I saw the sign in the window: Help Wanted.

There were two more years composed of an odd amalgam of jaw-popping boredom standing in front of a brass cash register and low, feverish excitement unpacking the apparatus created for illusionists. I always wished my father had still been alive when I met Harry in the magic shop back in 1919 or that he'd gotten to see me onstage in the glare of the footlights.

Houdini made every stagehand, rigger, prop boy, and silk-clad assistant swear to never—never to reveal—any of his secrets. I swore, too. Until now.

"MRS. DERWATT? So kind of you to meet me."

"Miss—if you want to get technical. Mrs. Derwatt was my mother, who's been dead since I was ten. But really, I prefer Leona. Just Leona."

"We have that in common. Using one name."

Emory flashed a thin-lipped grin at me, but I recalled when he'd been known as "The Professor" on the boards. A magician, he'd said—a medium. Years of working with Houdini taught me to be wary of mediums.

"I saw him perform—many times," Emory said. "His eyes were magnetic, you know. They had a glitter I've never seen in anyone else's. Looking into them was like gazing into a mirror reflecting sharp moonlight—a mirror on the bed of a dark sea." Emory's statement hung in the air for a moment, suspended in the cloud of cigarette smoke. "They said he hypnotized his audiences and there were—are—thousands of Spiritualists who believe he had that power. Among other talents, shall we say, of an even more occult nature."

6

Before I could answer, or even speculate about his motives, the waiter circled past, an eel swimming in the current of the nameless tune—more charivari than music—issuing from a three-piece jazz band. Emory pushed a scotch across the worn Formica tabletop toward me. How I hated cheap dirty bars with grimy floors, plastic ashtrays, and ungainly glassware. I didn't need the drink—not like poor Bess, wrecked by Harry's death—but what the hell, he was buying. He just didn't know I wasn't selling, I wasn't betraying: I was remembering....

THIRTY YEARS. I can't believe Houdini's been dead for thirty years. A lifetime ago. More than half the time I've lived and, except for me, all of them—the principals, anyhow—are gone. Bess, Sir Arthur—even that fraudulent bitch, Evelyn. That self-serving liar, that slut. I used to watch her sidelong glances, the intimate way she had of laying soft fingers on the iron-muscled forearm, laughing ... flirting. But Houdini proved she cheated during the séances and, like so many others, that she, too, was a fake. Still, he was almost unfailingly polite, and I'm almost certain he never succumbed—not to the likes of the she-demon medium. He couldn't have. Evelyn and her crowd were the ones who disappeared all those children ... and worse.

"God, I loved him."

Emory nodded. I saw his thin, elegant hand cant sideways to signal the waiter. There was a little magic, a little stardust in the gesture. Professionally trained; whatever status he might or might not have achieved on stage, not two in a hundred thousand men would use palm and fingers so eloquently. The drinks appeared, and I watched him slide the scotch so deftly into the circle of my reach the ice cubes barely moved. His skin was very bright against the black of the table and his tuxedo sleeves. I didn't look at his face. I watched his hands and thought about Harry.

"I want to show you some pictures."

They materialized on the table as if he'd wrung them from the air.

The short stack of photos lay face down alongside a small, tidy bundle of love letters tied with thin, lavender ribbon. I recognized them at once; my heart sped up, and I felt my pulse throbbing at my temple, but I made myself go calm, still, just as he'd taught me all those years ago.

MOST PEOPLE knew him as the consummate escape artist, but there were three distinct stages to his career and they mirrored the act he put on during his final years. First, the seemingly impossible feat. You could read the audience's collective reaction like newsprint: *How the hell did he do that?* This was the Houdini, manacled and chained, who escaped wooden packing cases tossed into icy rivers, fought his way out of straitjackets, prison cells, leather sacks, and—the *piece de résistance*—the Chinese Water Torture Cell. Next up, Houdini as conjurer supreme, the high priest of magic. Card tricks, sleight of hand, disappearing coins, elephants, and bejeweled assistants. And, finally, the debunker of fake mediums. He staged séances that trumped even the most lurid fiction. Men shuddered; women screamed, wept, fainted. Then he showed the audience how it was all done. He shared secrets, named names, enjoined local police to stand and affirm they'd smelled rats and detected trickery and sham—in every case, every time. When Spiritualists rose up and cried foul, they were shouted down. Newspapers headlined the gaudy rioting of the crowd, the atmosphere that crescendoed into circus pandemonium, the angry threats, the mediums' predictions of his imminent death, and his trumpeting rejoinder: "Say, listen, they're nothing but two-bit charlatans. They can chant and curse me 'til doomsday, then stick a thousand hatpins right through my picture trying to maim or kill me, but none of 'em could give me so much as even *one* lousy pimple." He was unafraid, defiant, a crusader ... and this was the Harry Houdini I met, worked for, and loved.

It wasn't hard to guess which picture Emory would show me first, and presto! *There it was*: a considerably thinner vision of myself, age twenty or so, decked out in a white summer frock and sporting a lacy parasol, standing next to forty-something Houdini (at five feet, five inches the tallest) who was, in turn, flanked by Bess. A typical 1920s studio portrait suggesting an afternoon at the seaside or a lakeshore excursion. Jolly companions. Three points of a mystical triangle ... but above us, swirling amid milky sky and puffy cumulus, a retinue of ghostly faces, all of them eerily blank-eyed and impassive, and all the more unnerving because each phantom had been a suicide. He was very interested in suicides....

I wondered if Emory knew about the small cemetery on the outskirts of Monte Carlo for those who lost at the gaming tables. In despair or drunkenness or both, they shot themselves or leapt from hotel balconies. The casino staff had a disconcerting habit of stuffing the pockets of those found with cash—as if they'd killed themselves over ruined love instead of wrecked finances. Houdini found it just before he'd gotten word his beloved mother had died. And wandering among weeds and unkempt stones, he told me he'd had his first premonition. Cecilia was gone; the telegram was an anticlimax.

"One of Houdini's little experiments, I presume," Emory said, tapping the edge of the photo with a fingernail. Fingernails were dangerous—underneath them, I knew, a variety of miniature implements and tools could be hidden—pencil lead, crayon, chalk, wax. He was creepy. *What did he really want from me?* Blackmail? He had the letters, but I wasn't going to let myself get distracted. I could string him along, too.

"Of *course* it was dummied," I said. "Sometimes he used double exposures—two plates, one with the live subjects, one with the disembodied—to create one photo. You must have seen the pictures of him sitting with Abraham Lincoln." I sipped the scotch, but I was suddenly cold, as if an icy wind gusted—that had been one of medium Eusapia Palladino's parlor tricks—and I scrutinized him more closely, forcing myself to concentrate. "Houdini made them to demonstrate how easily 'spirits' could appear in photographs. How naïve people—wounded with grief—could be duped into paying for another form of contact with loved ones who were dead. He exposed *all* their tricks, over and over—the phony slate-writing, telepathy, floating trumpets, blasts of arctic air, spirit-hands...."

"I LIKE the old walrus," Houdini said. "I really do, but anyone—well, practically anyone—can hoodwink him, and his influence is huge. Every newspaper here and across the pond writes up whatever twaddle he spouts." We were in the Manhattan townhouse on West 113th Street, and there was a scattering of clippings about Arthur Conan Doyle on his desk. "You'd think—he thinks—hell, I *thought*—the guy who dreamed up Sherlock Holmes would be the keenest observer on the planet." He grinned. "But children can fool him—in fact, they have.

That business with the fairy photographs...." He shook his head. "I thought we'd help him a little, nothing for him to be embarrassed about if we show him privately just how these things are done."

THE FAKE mediums maintained that strict linkage not only enhanced cosmic vibrations but, more importantly, *proved* that with their hands and feet accounted for, any manifestations had to come directly from spirit entities. I smiled thinking that, even though Houdini had said he was going to demonstrate how every effect could be accomplished by purely physical means and there was going to be absolutely *nothing* occult about this séance—because every bit was sheer conjuring—Sir Arthur was in for something of a shock.

Just like the phony trance artists, Houdini began with a prayer, his voice appropriately solemn even though, as I knew, he considered using prayer and hymns to connive believers the worst kind of blasphemy: *Can you imagine anything uglier than manipulating people's sincere belief in God to convince them you're genuine—the real, honest-to-Jesus ticket—when you're just about to scheme as many dollars as you can out of their pocketbooks? It's disgusting.*

The last "amen" intoned, the final strains of "Nearer My God to Thee" on the Victrola Houdini cranked up just before we'd taken seats faded, and there was a deep silence. I could feel Doyle's pulse against my fingertips. Houdini cleared his throat and said, "Are there any spirits here?"

Nothing.

"We have to concentrate ... there can be no resistance, no skepticism ... we have to open the portal, open ourselves."

Silence.

The merest dimming of the red lamp, but Sir Arthur's gaze was riveted on the circle of pale hands on the tabletop, and I wasn't sure he'd even noticed the growing darkness.

"If any spirits are here, we ask for a sign," Houdini said.

A tremendous boom—loud and startling as the crack of thunder. At the same time, the table rose upward swiftly and the red lamp went out with a hiss. I heard Doyle's sharp intake of breath, but his hand remained rooted in mine, even when we all lifted our arms as the wooden table tipped twice drunkenly then finally steadied itself, floating shoulder-high. Slowly, it rocked back and forth, finally settling down against the floor.

"Do you have a message for us?" Houdini breathed. A bell tinkled softly; in the dark, it was impossible to tell where the sound came from. "Who is the message for? Show us—we beg you, please."

Now there was a whispering sound—like the rustle of satin garments—and across the large room and out of the dark, the tiny faint outline of a dead white face swirled then moved slowly toward us, becoming larger and clearer.

"Who are you?" Houdini said. "Who is your message for?"

The eerie voice from the wavering figure was as mottled as if the thing's throat were choked with the dirt of the grave. "I ... have come," it rasped painfully, then trailed off. "So distant ... so hard...."

"Spirit, we can help you. Who are you? What is your message?"

"So much sorrow...."

"Do either of you recognize her? Leona? Sir Arthur?" She had long, wavy hair, dark glittering eyes; her mouth was a narrow slash. Doyle and I shook our heads.

"Give us a sign. Stroke the forehead of the one whose need to know brought you here. Make the sign of the cross." At the same instant, Doyle nearly jolted out of his seat, crying "Who *are* you?" A barely luminescent, distinct hand seemed to be already in the process of drawing away from the table and receding further into the darkness.

"That touch was ice cold," Doyle said. "Damn near startled me into losing my grip on your hands, Harry."

"You did well," Houdini said. "Your experience at so many séances over the years kept you steady. But I think there's more—let's find out who this woman is and what she wants to tell you," Houdini said. Then he addressed the spirit. "On the large desk near the standing globe, you'll find a bowl with warm paraffin; place your hands in it—then dip them into the bowl of cool water alongside. If you understand me, tap three times for yes."

Three sharp raps knocked against the wooden table.

"Excellent. Sir Arthur, did you wash the slates on all four sides as I told you before we started?"

"Yes, you gave me the damp sponge yourself, my dear boy."

11

"And they were completely blank on all four sides?"

"Yes."

"And you strung them from the cord we set up before we began?"

"Certainly. They're right where I hung them—just over our heads."
A stream of cold air blasted around us, and I felt Doyle's hand quake.

"Spirit, there is a set of locked slates—the same type children use in schoolrooms—dangling in midair just above this table. Kindly write your name and tell us why you're here. In particular, why you've come to see Sir Arthur Conan Doyle."

There was a brief pause ... then, scratching, like chalk writing on a blackboard.

"Do you hear that?" Doyle breathed.

"Yes," I said.

Houdini asked for quiet ... then a last prayerful invocation. "I'm going to use self-hypnosis to induce a trance state in myself, and I'm going to ask whatever spirits are present to rekindle the red lamp very, very slowly. And if they favor us, to give us a definite sign—the most definite sign possible from the other side. I'll say the prayer and Leona and Sir Arthur, you must entreat the spirit of this woman—or any others nearby. I'll say the prayer while you chant '*Donnez*.'" He took a deep breath. "Our Father who art in Heaven...."

Doyle and I kept a steady rhythm. "*Donnez, donnez ... donnez, donnez pour nous, donnez.*"

By the gleam of the light, we saw a tiny wisp—like spider web—slowly inch out from Houdini's mouth. Gradually, it thickened and seemed to grow heavier, pulling at him. He lay his head down on the table, and the ectoplasm twirled from between his lips and coiled over his chin until the large, faintly glowing mass puddled on the table. His eyes were closed; his breathing was so shallow Houdini appeared to have fainted.

"It's all right, Sir Arthur," I said. "You've seen me on stage with him, and I know what to do."

I called his name, we broke the circle, and I tapped his shoulder.

A few seconds later, his eyes fluttered open and he sat up.

"Are you dizzy? You look quite pale," Sir Arthur said. He turned to me. "I'm speaking as a doctor now, he's white as a sheet, and I think he ought to have a sip of brandy."

"He doesn't drink—"

"Well, he needs something. Let me feel his pulse."

"I'm all right ... really," Houdini said, but his smile appeared pasted on rather than genuine. "I must've been out of it. I was really under.... Did something happen?"

"LIGHTS PLEASE, Leona."

We all blinked when I switched on the first of the Tiffany lamps. Doyle hovered over the magician. "You're still milk pale, and your pulse is thready, Harry."

Houdini waved him away. "I'm all right. Leona, fetch the brandy—for Sir Arthur." He grinned. "And then you and I will show him how it was all done."

"I'VE SAID it a hundred times—whether you know it or not, you've got occult power—it's the only explanation for how you pull off those stunts of yours."

"All purely physical, Sir Arthur. Nothing supernatural, I assure you."

"On stage, perhaps, but I know fainting when I see it, and I know an irregular heartbeat when I feel it."

"In good light at a patient's bedside, undoubtedly. But not here—not tonight—and certainly not when fakirs claim they have control over their heartbeats." He pulled a small, hard India rubber ball from deep inside the hollow of his armpit and playfully bounced it to me. I caught it and walked it through my fingers before I palmed it and it appeared to have vanished. Houdini and I both laughed when Doyle's face registered surprise, his mouth hanging open like a hinged box you could've used to trap woodcocks. "One merely has to squeeze the hidden ball," Harry explained, "and since the circulation to the fingers is diminished, it makes it seem as though the pulse is slower or weakened."

"Hidden in the axilla—the underarm, you say?"

"Right. Now, let's sit at the séance table again."

With the lights on, we sat down and linked hands and feet. "Look under the table—what do you see?"

"Same as before, my foot is right on top of your toes."

"Look up," Houdini said, and a second later the tinkling bell rang.

"Look again." Doyle dived underneath and we all laughed. Houdini had withdrawn his foot from the shoe, and the bell—grasped between his naked toes sticking out of a brown half-sock—was ringing wildly. "Special shoes, Sir Arthur. They have steel caps so that, as the sitter, you can't tell my foot's not under yours."

"Huh!"

Houdini slid his foot back into the shoe. "Let's show him the apparition—now watch closely, Sir Arthur."

The red bulb in the sconce guttered out, but Doyle's gaze was riveted on the tiny white blur of a face—seemingly the dimension of a demitasse saucer—that appeared in the furthest corner of the library then slowly came nearer, gaining in size and clarity the closer it came to the séance table.

When it was hovering above Doyle, its winding sheet brushing his shoulder, the polar chill blustered menacingly around us, and just before the spirit receded into sparkling mist, the luminescent hand traced the cross on Doyle's forehead.

"Well?"

"You've told me it's trickery, but my dear fellow, I'm sitting here live as Parliament, and can't say I've a clue how you've done it." He blinked owlishly—more Watson than Holmes to my way of thinking.

The incandescent lights came on—this time Houdini didn't bother with asking me to get up—as he stepped on one of the buttons hidden under the carpet.

"There are several ways to create an apparition," Houdini said, "and I've used them all. Sometimes—depending on how many people are participating—I (or a confederate) get up. In that case, I don a mask and a black satin robe streaked with phosphorescent paint, and just cavort around the room as necessary. Tonight, though, Leona let go of my hand, and I used magician's thread to pull the mask and drapery—which is French veiling boiled in olive oil and water, then luminesced—closer to the table."

"I saw it float near the ceiling—"

"Yes, the thread is rigged through eyehooks up there." He pointed. "And over by the standing globe, and the bookshelves," Houdini said.

"And that icy draft—a fan, I presume? One that's quite silent, I might add."

Houdini shook his head and grinned. "Using my free hand, I took a thin, black rubber glove from my pocket—where there was also an ice cube nestling." He took out what was now melted to the size of a small cork and tossed it onto the table. "Notice one side of the glove is painted with phosphorous—so when I wave the black side, I can create the chilled breeze, but when I made the sign of the cross, I turned the glove so you could see its glow, and of course it was cold—in one's imagination the rime of the tomb—when I touched you with it."

"Marvelous."

"The ectoplasm is a regurgitation trick."

"I say, that's foul."

Houdini chuckled. "People have been paying money for centuries to watch sword swallowers, stone eaters, and fakirs who imbibe poison. Did you know back in 1650 there was a man named Floram Marchand who advertised that he could produce any liquor his audience named in his vomitus? A few hours before his performance he merely drank water infused with color from soaking Brazil nuts—naturally, he started his routine with the darker beverages."

"The swallowing business brings to mind the time some stupid fop shoved a billiard ball down his gullet on a bet at my club. He did it three times—won a potful of money, too. But then this chap drank a few more brandies and tried it again on a double or nothing wager, and it got stuck. More's the pity, I was the sole doctor nearby—not only was I an eye specialist back when I had my practice, but naturally I hadn't been on a ward in *years*. We nearly had to break the poor fool's jaw to get the damn thing out."

"I learned the art from a circus lad when I was ten—and one practices by using a very small potato on a string."

The slates were taken down and Houdini demonstrated how, with a faked flap, the message he'd already written was concealed so that while Doyle thought he was washing all four sides, he never came close to seeing it. Slates, the magician told him, could be tricked in a hundred ways—by exchanging them over the sitter's head or under the table, or with an accomplice hidden nearby. The sound of the writing was achieved by Houdini's fingernail scratching a piece of slate glued under the table. In fact, that was even easier than concealing writing done on the sly in a pocket or behind one's back using a well-known magical device, a Swami—a kind of miniature clip—that went under the fingernail and held tiny bits of chalk, crayon, or lead pencil. "That takes actual practice to do well," Houdini snickered. "In the dime museums, I knew lots of armless folk who could manage everything from picking up drinking glasses to writing with their toes. I can do that too, in a pinch, if I have to put the slate on the floor to chalk out a spirit message. If I'm using, say, my pockets, I can write with either hand—and also backwards—if I need to show the message using mirrors."

The table itself could be levitated with clips attached to his belt, with his knees, his feet ... or by means of a silver ring he wore that had a notch that fitted to a straight pin hammered into the tabletop. "And, of course, there are many other ways to tilt a table—and clever mediums combine methods and change them up to keep the sitters off balance."

"And you say some of these mediums actually go to magic shops and have apparatus constructed?"

"Not *some*, Sir Arthur. *All*."

"I worked at Martinka's—that's where I met Mr. Houdini—and I can vouch for what he says. You wouldn't believe how many mediums were on the client list. There was even a secret catalogue of conjuring effects mediums could use that got passed around—a lot. They used it to cover their tracks when they ordered. It had everything from—"

"There's also something," he interrupted, "called a Blue Book, Sir Arthur—only instead of listing the names of upper-crusters and the society gang like that Debrett's peerage you have over in England—it's got a roster of suckers. People that mediums have successfully hoodwinked, like rich, lonely widows who are ripe for further fleecing. The East coast version alone has more than two thousand names."

"But, my dear Houdini, I know that some mediums will bamboozle now and then—but only when their genuine powers are momentarily in, uh ... in remission," Sir Arthur said.

Houdini shook his head. "Tell him, Leona; tell him how they laugh about the gulls. They call them 'shut-eyes,'" he said. Then he showed Doyle the wax hand he'd asked the spirit to cast. It was done with another rubber glove filled with water—though air would work, too.

"But the wrist opening is too small for any human to pull away his hand without breaking the mold."

"That's where the water comes in—the fraudulent medium only has to empty the glove and it can be removed with no problem whatsoever."

"But Houdini, I have such a spirit hand in my possession and I assure you it wasn't faked. Just because you can replicate a trick, that doesn't mean that's how it was done." Doyle seemed very proud of his logic. "You can't be saying—surely, they're not all fakes."

"Sir Arthur, let me put it to you this way. If you threw me and a *thousand* Spiritualist mediums—all of us wearing handcuffs and locked inside roped trunks—into the East River, I'd be the *only* one who came up."

Doyle sputtered a little, but nothing more on the subject was said. The man was a guest in his house and Houdini let it drop, too—but I think they both knew it was the beginning of the end of their friendship.

IT WAS the third time we met at the same down-at-heels, west side bar. Emory had on the same rusty tuxedo, but for the first time, I was aware that the jacket was tight—as if he'd gained weight—and the cuffs were slightly frayed in the place where magicians concealed the hocus-pocus part of their tricks. His cheeks and chin didn't look fuller, and I remembered reading that the first place gain or loss showed was the face. What did he have under the jacket? And why was he continually playing down his role as a medium?

"The usual?" he asked.

"No, I feel like something breezy. A Tom Collins." The drink bars were built on—the cheapest shot of weak gin topped up with lemonade and seltzer. The breeze I wanted was interior, one that would keep my head clear.

"F'christ's sake, it's barely the first week of March," he said.

"Are you saying I should keep to the rules—like only wearing white shoes after Memorial Day?" I smiled. "I didn't think you were such a stickler about etiquette, Emory."

"Not me, have whatever the hell you want."

"Thank you, I will." I glanced around at the haze of cigarette smoke, the sweaty dancers gyrating to the seedy band, the steam radiators hissing overhead. "And it may be March, but with the fug in this joint, it might as well be July." The short stack of photos was in evidence tonight, and I could see the edge of the love letter bundle protruding under the Professor's lapel. *How sweet, he's got them next to his heart.* The only question was which little group of artifacts he'd produce first to prod me about. His hand flashed over his breast. *Ah, the letters.*

"Got anything to say for yourself, Leona?"

Bess was dead; Houdini was dead. Did this fool think he could blackmail me? Intimidation, maybe, but it wasn't going to work. "Since you have these, I'm guessing you know that after Harry died, Bess found all kinds of letters—and when they were from women, she called them in one at a time and the maid would tell each of them 'Mrs. Houdini is not at home to you today, but she left these.' Then Julia, the housekeeper, would hand over the letters—tied in bundles just like that one—and the 'lady friend' would depart. I was called, but I didn't take the letters I wrote—I left them there," I said. "I guess Julia hid them and they got moved around from pillar to post and you—or someone you know—came up with them. Could that someone be Arthur Ford?"

He hid it well, but I detected the faintest grimace on his face, the slight cringe he gave. There'd be more bravado in a second or two.

"As a matter of fact, I did get them from Ford," he said.

"Dubious. The Arthur Ford I knew—and know of now—wouldn't share a used toothpick after a meal, even if you picked up the check."

"Just the same—"

"Can it, why don't you? It doesn't matter where you got the damn letters—not to me." All right, he took the bait about Ford. Magician, my ass. Ford—that cheap, swindling medium—must be a rival of Emory's. And of course, he could best the lying bastard if he suddenly came up with the real inside dope—the kind of information one of Houdini's closest confidantes had to share. I stood up suddenly and excused myself to go powder my nose—a quaint euphemism as we both knew, for going to the ladies' room to take a piss. It would buy me a few minutes and I could think about the truth regarding Arthur Ford—and better, come up with a plan for what I'd brew up to tell him. What was it the shrinks called it? Confabulation ... yes.

ARTHUR FORD. Miraculously, even this crumby tavern did have a long, mirrored vanity table—though it was draped with stained fabric and littered with dirty ashtrays and lipstick-smeared, crumpled tissues. I sat on a dingy pink-skirted stool and lit a cigarette. Nose powdering and makeup repair could wait. *Arthur Ford.*

That four-flusher. Houdini would've had the Reverend's head in a handbasket—same as Evelyn's—in fifteen minutes. And just like Evelyn, even after he was exposed, people still flocked to his séances. The only difference was that Ford was still alive, had even been reinstated in the Spiritualist church. Unbelievable.

Houdini always said Conan Doyle was dangerous—because people listened to him—and while he may have been a top-drawer literary man who considered himself very capable of ferreting out chicanery in the séance room, he was so biased in favor of proving the dead did *actually* communicate, he couldn't see past that point of view.

Okay, it was his religion—and he was as devout as any priest or nun—but Doyle never questioned Spiritualism as a faith that began as a series of pranks carried out by two girls in upstate New York in the 1840s—not even forty years later, when one of them confessed the scheme and how it began with secretly dropping apples tied to strings and ended with using their toe joints to rap the floor and make the spirits answer questions in darkened rooms.

Despite what Doyle and other rabid Spiritualists thought, Houdini really did understand why so many held beliefs as unwavering as his father's—the scholar, Rabbi Weiss. Houdini himself genuinely spent years looking for the tiniest glimpse of an afterlife that included speaking with the dead. *Years.* But instead of the contact he and millions of others sought, he'd found nothing but shamming. Deft fakery, mediocre conjuring, and badly done bunkum—the whole gamut. Doyle pooh-poohed Houdini's role, but in truth, Houdini always admitted that as a pro, it was more likely he could spot deception—and even *he* had to observe closely and think long and hard about the effects produced by some of the more skilled mediums.

Ford. I caught a glimpse of myself rolling my eyes just thinking about him. If you want to know the truth, I blamed Sir Arthur for siccing the fake medium on all of us. Within two weeks of Houdini's death on Halloween 1926, Conan Doyle and Bess were corresponding. Guess who wrote first? Ford was already one of his lordship's darlings—yet another in the long series of charlatans he declared had genuine powers. He shipped Ford back to New York, where the good Reverend campaigned in earnest to get hold of the secret code Houdini laid out for her—the code *Rosabelle, Believe*—that would let Bess know her Harry had truly come back from the dead.

ARTHUR FORD had been caught in that particular hoax by means of a canny reporter, plus two witnesses hidden out of sight—but not out of hearing—and, better still, a Dictaphone that recorded the whole shabby conversation. Times had changed, and I found myself wondering if Emory had some kind of miniature device under his coat. Times had changed and Harry was gone, and now it was time to give this Emory, this son of a bitch, an earful. It would be payback for what Ford had done to Bess—what he'd done to me.

Emory was no slouch either when it came to the phony medium biz—he was just lucky he'd merely been a failing magician when Houdini was alive and didn't take up the clairvoyant act 'til after Harry was gone. As far as I knew, Emory had never been exposed publicly, but I'd kept an ear to the ground, and one of my old pals from the conjuring world told me about Emory's line. His specialty was materializing the dead—only instead of bringing back wailing infants to grieving mothers or long-lost brothers, he focused on lonely old widowers.

With the hefty fees he collected, he paid shady detectives to dig up information and cheap prostitutes to disguise themselves in the dim lamplight of his back bedroom as the widowers' dead wives. It had only backfired one time—in New Orleans where that particular shut-eye got so overexcited at the prospect of clasping his dead bride once again, the old beaver had a heart attack. They dragged his body to the nearby docks, but the fancy-girl was so unnerved, she got drunk and told a tableful of barflies, swearing she was done for good with Emory's bring-back-the-dead tricks. If the whole charade weren't so pathetic, it would be funny as hell. At any rate, I heard the local cops took a huge bite out of the wad of folding green Emory had been collecting for six months or more, then suggested it was time for him to vaporize—dissipate like smoke or steam on a river—never to be seen in the Big Easy again.

I PAWED through the detritus in my purse. I don't know why smokers always need larger handbags—but we do. There was a gold cigarette case I carried everywhere and seldom used—and certainly not in front of Emory. The engraving read:

Mirable Visu. Wonderful to Behold
To Leona—On Her Special Day—from Harry
March 22nd 1923

I set it aside and dug deeper into the abyss. Someday someone will have a brainstorm and make the insides of women's handbags with brightly colored linings—apple green and daffodil and periwinkle—so they can find what they're looking for without feeling like they're descending one layer at a time into a coal mine.

I RETCHED a little. My hand instinctively went to my mouth, but nothing came up. My gag reflex wasn't what it used to be. Out of practice. I took a deep breath this time and began swallowing first the little rubber sack, then the thin length of tubing, making sure the open end was properly placed under my tongue.

The easiest way to be certain the booze went straight down the chute and into the bag would be if I drank from a straw. Have to be careful about my speech—aside, that is, from sounding as if I'm schnockered.

"THOUGHT for a minute there, you fell in—or ran out," Emory said.

I shrugged. "No fear of either. The ladies' loo is on the second floor, and the window opens out over a cobblestone alley. Besides, I'm completely rusty when it comes to vanishing."

"That's too bad."

I finished the drink, head tilted way back, in two long swallows; then glanced at Emory and he signaled the waiter immediately. "That Tom Collins was watery as hell—ask the bartender to make this one a double," I said, putting the empty glass on the serving tray. *If you fooled thousands of people night after night as Harry's assistant and number one box jumper,* and *played spy for him going out to investigate chary mediums—putting on disguises and pretending to be a distraught widow or an anxious wife—you can fool one greed-sotted idiot. Time to act, Leona, so make it good, make it good as smoke and mirrors.*

THE WAITER brought my sugary concoction and his brandy.

I lifted the glass to "clink" against Emory's. "Cheers," I said. "And thanks. Next round is on me."

My tongue felt clumsy and I was conscious of a minor sibilance that wasn't quite a lisp, but seemed very distinct to me. I knew from the brief run-through I'd practiced in the bathroom my speech definitely sounded more natural with the narrow pale-beef colored tube inside the gutter of my cheek, but it would have looked absurd to line up the drinking straw with the extreme right corner of my mouth. It had been too many years since I'd used a similar device and, unlike my mentor when he did the famous Needle Trick, I couldn't move it adroitly. In order to shift the tiny, flexible cylinder over my back molars and under my tongue, I had to poke it into position with a finger. *Misdirection I can manage; or surreptitious movement when he's looking anywhere else—at the table, the tin ceiling, the sax player, his wristwatch, my tits—hell, anywhere.*

It was a good plan—pretending to be tipsy and chummy and spilling beans that wouldn't matter much even to a bean counter—in order to find out what Emory's real agenda was. Conversational misdirection.

It *was* a good plan—and it might have worked if I'd hatched out a contingency plot. Or maybe it wouldn't have. Magicians are all about control that masquerades as surprise and they're much better at it than their assistants.

Emory swirled the brandy—a very small one—drank it off and put the snifter onto the waiter's tray. "Mr. Emory? It's almost eleven. And, um, Sam told me to tell you the band is off in about ten minutes—and you're on as soon as you can set up."

"HENCE the tuxedo?" I said as casually as I could manage.

Emory grinned. "You left too early both times you were here before."

"How long have you had the gig?"

"Coupla months. Thursdays. It's just the one show a night when the band guys take their long break for three-quarters of an hour or so. I'm on for maybe twenty, twenty-five minutes."

"What's in the act?"

"Little of this, little bit of that." He shrugged. "Depends on the crowd—and my mood."

"Pretty small venue. Card tricks, coins?"

"Sometimes," he said. "But I'm glad you're here tonight because I'm doing much longer and bigger shows on March 24th and April 6th—they're weekend spots, Friday and Saturday. That's what I meant before when I said it's too bad you're out of practice. I thought you might want to work with me ... you know, in honor of Harry."

I felt the vein pulsing in my throat. Houdini was actually born on March 24th—but he always celebrated his birthday on April 6th. People weren't really sure why. Since he was originally from Budapest, it could have been as simple as the difference between the Julian and Gregorian methods of timekeeping. Except I didn't think so. I thought it was on account of something called Gauss's mathematic formula to reckon the Jewish calendar. It was why my cigarette case was inscribed March 22nd—my secret birthday, Harry called it. I was pretty sure Emory didn't know about our private context, but magician or medium, what the hell was he up to?

"I'll think about it," I said.

Then he sprang away toward the stage and disappeared behind the makeshift curtain.

ABOUT FIVE minutes later, the bartender hurried toward the stage, still wiping his hands on the cotton towel that hung from his belt, and harrumphed into the microphone. "Ladies and gentlemen, tonight—during the interlude—the Blue Moon Café proudly presents magic and mystification ... the amazing ... Emory!"

The tavern lamps blacked out briefly, then simultaneously there was an explosive pop and a bright flash that transitioned into a puff of smoke. The vapor dissipated; a cone of dull purple light shot with sparkling motes like stars gradually grew brighter and, in the center, standing very tall and straight, his arms folded across his chest, Emory suddenly appeared.

WITH PATTER and set-ups, I knew there wasn't much he could do in twenty minutes, but he had a nice little spirit act of thematically linked tricks.

"I call this, 'Disappearing Scotch—or Johnny Walker Takes a Hike.'" He flashed a wide grin—not unlike John Barrymore—to humor the crowd, begin to win them to his side. "Now I realize it may not be the most popular trick—especially in a bar—but I guarantee that if you watch closely, you can find a way to make the waiter re-tabulate your bill—or you can figure out how to stop paying for drinks for everyone else at your table. Those pikers." Another grin.

There was a small rectangular stand alongside him. He held up a bottle of Johnny Walker Red and uncapped it, inhaling its aroma. "It's the good stuff, all right."

He poured a hefty double and lifted it again, then he passed the glass to the guy sitting at the first table on the right. "Just taste that for me would you, Sir? It *is* scotch, correct?"

"Yeah."

"Whoa, I said, 'taste.'" He held up the glass again.

Chuckles.

He retrieved the glass and rapidly took the two or three paces back to his stand. "I didn't intend for it to *disappear* down that guy's throat. Well, we'll add a little more of the good stuff." He sniffed. "It's still scotch."

"All right, watch closely. Because, my dear friend," he said to the taster, "the next round—out of this bottle—is for you."

He waved a small, thin handkerchief over the tumbler. Flicked it away ... and the tumbler was gone. "Oh well," he said. "I guess not—because *you* don't have a glass."

Smattering of applause, but you could feel a little interest in the room. There'd be fewer idle chatterers and more quiet spectators for the next trick.

"We all know Houdini was the greatest escape artist of all time. And who wouldn't want to trade places with him? When he was alive, of course."

Polite laughter.

"If you'd like to have a chance to do just that—to trade places with the master—please pass up your business cards. Ladies, I don't mean to be unfair to you—so if you have a calling card, feel free to join in."

People dug into wallets and handbags, and the relay forward commenced. Emory's table now held two tall white candles in holders set at least thirty inches apart and, leaning against each red lacquered candlestick, an 8 x 10 ornate picture frame.

He sorted through the cards. "John Jones?"

"Here."

"Are you sure that's not an alias?" Laughter. "No, it isn't—because we've never met before, have we?"

"Nope."

"Please step forward to the stage. And—" He glanced through the small stack again. "Alice Faye? You don't know either of us? Right, come on up here with Mr. Jones. Miss Faye didn't pass a visiting card—she sent up a business card—and by the way, Jones, it's nicer than yours—hers is engraved." Laughter. "Mr. Jones, would you please sign the back of your card? And Miss Faye, here's a box of matches; while he's signing his John Hancock, would you light the candles behind the picture frames? Very good. Now turn both picture frames around."

They stood either side of Emory, and he held up the frames one at a time, showing both sides. "This silver one, as you can see, is empty." He casually removed its black velvet backing and held it up so the audience could see through the glass. "And the second—with the brass frame—on the left, has a photo of the great Harry Houdini. Also signed. And I venture to guess his signature is probably worth a lot more than yours, Jones ... but we'll proceed anyhow."

He picked up an ordinary business envelope from the table and opened the flap.

He showed the audience both sides—the front was stamped and addressed:

> **Mr. Harry Houdini**
> **278 West 113th St.**
> **New York City, New York**

"After all," Emory said, "you wouldn't want your card—or your soul—to wind up in Machpelah Cemetery ... at least not yet." The audience laughed.

"Hold up the card and show the audience that it's yours and that you signed it. Very good. Now place it in the envelope and seal it—that's right, give it a good lick—then set it on the pile of cards on the table—the ones from all those unlucky folks who aren't going to get to trade places with Houdini like you are." Emory held up the envelope, flourished the cards, and set both down again. He stood aside.

"Now, Miss Faye is going to hand you the empty picture frame, and I want you to put the envelope—which contains your business card—inside the silver frame. Excellent ... and each of you please turn the frames around so the velveteen backs face the audience."

Emory stood in front of the table while the two impromptu assistants stood on either side. He placed his hands palms together and, inclining his head down a little, closed his eyes. The lights dimmed so that in the dusk of the tavern the candle flames appeared brighter, their reflections dancing in the polished brass and silver.

Then he suddenly clapped his hands twice.

And both frames fell over onto the table.

A few people jumped.

Emory smiled.

"I believe, even from beyond the grave, Houdini has escaped yet *again*—and his photo has changed places with your business card, Mr. Jones—but let's check, shall we?"

"Mr. Jones, please turn the silver frame around and show the front to the audience. And, Miss Faye, please turn the brass frame around and show its front."

"Holy shit, the envelope is gone!" one of his friends called out. "And your card's in the brass picture frame, John!"

"And Houdini is in the silver—where he belongs," Emory said, taking the brass frame from the girl and swiftly opening its back and offering it like a tray. "Pick up the card ... and it's the card you signed, isn't it Mr. Jones?"

Jones looked astonished. He looked at his signature then held it up for the audience to see.

There was clapping, some whistling. Emory made as if to leave the stage.

"One more!" Someone shouted and the audience took it up.

Emory held his hands up.

"All right. Can someone lend me a gold wedding ring? You'll get it right back, so if you're happily married, there's absolutely nothing to worry about.... Ma'am? You'd like to lend us your ring for this trick?"

A young woman—not more than twenty-three or twenty-four, I guessed—at one of the tables near the front nodded and Emory went to her. "Betty, you say your name is? Stand up so everyone can see you, Betty." She looked like a Gimbels salesgirl or a secretary—hair smoothed and pulled back in a fake tortoiseshell barrette, maroon collared sweater, and a tiny, dark-wine and pale-jade scarf tied around her neck. And that's your husband sitting next to you?"

She nodded again. "Yes, Joe," she said quietly.

"How long have you been married? Fourteen months? Tell me, is this the first time you've ever taken off your ring?"

"Yes—except once. We had a fight."

"A tiff," Joe corrected.

"He was out all night."

"Are you bringin' that up again? F'chrissakes, I toldja, my cousin Bobby's truck had a flat we couldn't get fixed on account of the holiday and we was stuck up in Binghamton. In a snowstorm, f'chrissakes."

"Joe, your language."

Part of being a good magician—or medium—is being able to sight-read people. While the audience watched this charming bit of repartee unfold into household drama, Emory maintained his emcee status. He never let the two of them wander out of his control—but he could have vanished an elephant while the newlyweds carried on.

"Binghamton is pretty far upstate," he put in. "Couple hundred miles. And much colder. Deer hunting?"

"Huh! Howja know?" Joe said.

"You mentioned the holiday...."

"See, this guy—he gets it."

"But you didn't bring home no deer, Joe. Three days and no call and no deer," Betty said, her voice trailing off.

The crowd erupted into hoots and snickers that might have come from a laugh track. Emory stepped in. "But everything has been great since then, right?"

Betty, clearly familiar with contestants' behavior on TV game shows, nodded enthusiastically.

"Excellent. Now, we need to borrow a couple of things from Sam. I trust most of you know Sam—bartender extraordinaire and the owner of the Blue Moon Café." Smattering of applause.

SOMEWHERE in the midst of this tête-à-tête between Emory and the happily wedded couple, and the tiny *frisson* between Emory and his audience, I began to hear the sound of a baby crying fretfully. At first, dazed on the alcohol I'd shipped into my system earlier that night, and the shock from Emory's unexpected performance, I looked around seeking the source of that thin, hiccoughing wail. But it was a bar—alternatively noisy and hushed, deeply shadowed in the corners, garishly lit with neon signs that sucked up visual purple and created temporary blind spots, hazy with smoke and body heat. It was nearly midnight—surely no one had lugged an infant in here—and to what purpose? For a second, I thought I was reading someone's psychic aura: perhaps young Betty was pregnant. I glanced at her more pointedly and decided she didn't have the look of someone gestating.

Still that sub-sound—which to me was very loud—persisted.

At times, it seemed to wind among the tables and drift from the darker recesses of the old pressed-tin ceiling, and it began to worry me a great deal. It changed in tone from low whimpering to plaintive shriek and back again, over and over, and it whittled at me 'til I wanted to scream.

Then, abruptly, it broke off—as sharply as a smothered yelp—the sound a puppy makes when its sadistic master has just delivered an impulsive kick to its midsection and it fears another. The weeping—followed by the ominous silence—unnerved me.

I'm afraid I didn't stay for Emory's finale—I'd already figured the trick he had in the works was his version of an old standard. Betty's wedding ring would appear to have been accidentally smashed (when in fact the bar's ice mallet was used to break a duplicate). A confederate (in this case, Sam) would be prevailed upon to give the young woman and her highly irritated husband an amelioration—champagne, most likely. Emory would surreptitiously take the broken ring pieces and wrap them in a tiny bit of flash paper—there would be a bright flare and all would disappear in smoke and flame. Emory would appear to be stricken and offer to pay out of his own pocket for another, more expensive vintage from Sam's stock. Emory would pour them each a first glass.

Then, when (seemingly amid apologizing, he made things worse by intimating the ring clearly wasn't *genuine* 14k) he'd gotten both Joe *and* Betty heated up to the proper pitch, he'd shatter the bottle he'd just poured their Dom Perignon from and out would fly a small white dove with Betty's shiny golden ring—intact and restored—tied around its neck on a fluttering silk ribbon.

AFTER I LEFT the café, instead of going home, I found myself wandering the streets until, completely lost in thought, I saw I was standing in front of 278 West 113th.

Bess had sold their huge old brownstone, and it was completely dark that night. It had the look of emptiness ... abandonment ... desolation.

No one had lived here for years.

I supposed little, if anything—personal *or* magical—that'd been Harry's remained. And the urge to ferret out memorabilia—overlooked or forgotten—wasn't what drew me in. At least I don't think so. Maybe it was the earlier talk of Houdini's upcoming birthday or the invocation I sensed in Emory's trick with the autographed photo. Maybe it was just seeing Emory over these last few weeks. Or maybe it was because, like a few other trusted associates, Bess and Harry took me in. Whatever it was, it certainly wasn't overly difficult for the premier assistant of the former greatest escape artist in the world to fashion a quick pick-lock from the metal nail file in my purse and open the cellar door just below street level.

THE MOMENT I stepped inside, I wondered what on earth had kept me out of his house all these years. But, of course, I knew that answer. Before tonight, I'd had no need: Houdini had been coming back to me—and me alone—for decades.

SUMMONING

It was more than curiosity. More than just wondering how the once grand, sparkling chandeliers would look—draped and muffled with sagging cloth, or naked and dimmed with the accumulation of passing years and the work of spiders whose own webs had gathered velvety dust, as well. Would I find the tile in the great sunken bathtubs cracked and blackened with mold? A wardrobe with its broken door hanging like a crippled shutter; inside, on its wooden floor, a scuffed-kid dancing shoe lying on one side—its frayed ribbons creased with time and dirt?

That first night, I wandered in the lower rooms by aid of matches and whatever mottled street light crept through the windows—there was no moon. But after that, I brought along what phony mediums used to call a bell reader. In the dark of a séance parlor, the hooded lamp enabled them to identify the contents of letters inside ostensibly locked curio boxes, then pass on the information—as if those messages came from the dead. For my purposes, it kept errant beams and flickers from being seen through the windows by vigilant neighbors, would-be acolytes, and beat patrolmen.

NOBODY—not Bess, not the secretaries, not the investigators he hired, nor the assistants—ever called it "Houdini's place" or spoke the full address on West 113th or referred to it as "the Houdinis' house." It was always just "278." *Meet me at 278. I'll be at 278. I'm leaving 278 in time to take the noon train west and, after that, you can catch up with the troupe in Chicago.* Back in the day, the place was always a hive of activity. Phones rang, deliverymen stormed the entries, and librarians cataloged books and articles, clipped news stories, and edited his manuscripts. Seamstresses kept their machines humming, stitching finishing touches on costumes. It was so lively, in fact *and* in my memory, I found the silence now oppressive.

I sat on the thick floorboards of the parlor one evening not long after my first foray inside 278, little scenes of the past unfurling like scarves he pulled from thin air: Bess and one of the prop girls, back from a shopping trip, crowding the foyer with noise and hilarity, sporting live twin chameleons on leashes; Houdini, trying a new effect in the basement workroom and, after what sounded like a rocket explosion, emerging into the kitchen, his grin sheepish behind a coating of soot; Bess tossing his gray fedora into the front hall—their private signal when they quarreled, which meant she was still miffed and he was not yet welcome; the staff chuckling, because everyone knew he'd pace the neighborhood streets and keep trying until the hat no longer came flying back at him and he was once again in her good graces.

To reminisce—even for a moment—was to conjure up the smell of good, honest Old-World cooking; the sight glimpsed through icy windows of Bess's annual Christmas tree—towering, beautiful in its simplicity and candleglow; the sounds of German music and Yiddish jokes and American radio and sparkling laughter, high and sweet.

Now, the air was dead. There was nothing but the smell of dust, the sight of barren rooms and stripped walls, the sound of freezing rain cascading down the chimneys and pelting broken window glass.

THERE'D ALWAYS been talk about Harry's occult powers. Sir Arthur was the biggest proponent of that theory, but plenty of others were convinced his escapes were achieved by Houdini's actual dematerialization from the jails, the milk can, the Chinese Water Torture Cell. The more he denied it by declaring everything he did was accomplished solely by physical means, the more they believed his statements were a blind to hide his supernatural gifts.

In October of 1926, not long before he died, Houdini's friend Joe Dunninger picked him up. As the car was traversing Central Park, Houdini asked him to go back to 278. No, he hadn't forgotten anything; he just wanted to go back, he insisted. Harry stood in the rain for a long time, staring up at the brownstone. After a while, he got back into the car. He was crying. "Joe," he said, "I'll never see my house again." And he was right.

Then there were the stories about how two of three plaster copies of the portrait bust he had commissioned for his tomb mysteriously broke in the immediate weeks after his death. Stories that for years he wakened in the night calling out, "Mama, is that you? Are you here?" And, about how one of the secret codes by which Houdini would make his return from the afterlife known was penciled into a copy of Roget's Thesaurus the magician gave to writer Arthur Hilliar; but three weeks after his death, Hilliar—who'd referenced the book for many years before that—noted that the code had suddenly and inexplicably disappeared. All that was left of the inscription was Houdini's signature.

In the weeks right before and just after he died, friends reported pictures of Houdini that jumped from walls for no apparent reason. Bess—and several others—talked about mirrors abruptly exploding or plummeting.

But what were all these incidents—mere coincidence I called them, and so would've Harry—to what I'd shared with him? In 278, now a ravaged shell of its former glory, I laughed.

For years, I'd played the girl in the crystal ball—a trick Harry always had fun with. To the audience, it appeared disembodied hands wrote messages, a woman clad in flowing robes spoke prophecy and read minds while pale gray mist swirled about her. A novelty back in its day, the effect was not unlike the visions in the wicked witch's crystal that taunted Dorothy in *The Wizard of Oz*.

But I was here in his parlor, and I didn't need props to summon him. I didn't even need to speak out loud, but I did.

"Harry, the children still cry out for you," I said.

Then I waited, silent as granite, patient as a stone saint.

IT WAS Evelyn, the phony medium, and that miserable husband of hers, Fred Trilby, who disappeared those immigrant English boys. Even Doyle—their pal—wrote and asked what happened, and he was satisfied with an airy reply. The child in question had been shipped back to its family and the oh-so-charming couple just didn't know his whereabouts. End of investigation. End of queries about any other missing British boys.

Evelyn had been, at that point, a thorn in Houdini's side for several years. "A woman," he said, "who would drag her dead brother from the grave to gain social prominence would do anything."

And he was right.

He was part of a committee for the *Scientific American* asked to either verify her psychic talents or expose her fakery. Quite a task—

when half the committee was boarding cozily *chez* Trilby, feasting on lamb and charlotte russe for luncheon and dinner, and the rest were either sleeping with Evelyn—or trying to.

I don't say that Evelyn was the first fraudulent medium to use sex to her advantage during a séance—but she was better at it, *and* better-looking. Younger, too, than most of the harridans I visited undercover and Houdini unmasked. I don't think she was even thirty when she came to the magazine's attention around 1924 via our old friend, Sir Arthur. Those damn rabid Spiritualists lived in each other's pockets, so if you ask me, it was on account of Evelyn that the last vestiges of cordiality between Doyle and Houdini dissipated. Worse still, prodded by their predictions the magician would die soon, those crazed fanatics made sure the prophecy was fulfilled.

And the world lost one of its great lights.

"WHAT'S the scoop on her, Leona?"

Houdini had sent me ahead to Boston that June. It was much hotter than I expected, and I'd just kicked off my shoes and peeled my stockings when he phoned my hotel room.

"I did a lot of digging—and some of this you probably know already, but I'll just go through my notes."

"Ready when you are."

I grinned, visualizing him at the desk in 278, his chair tilted back, one hand behind his head, his feet propped up on the shiny mahogany. He'd relax and just listen until I hit my stride with the new info.

"She was born in New Jersey, moved to the Boston area when she was a tyke. Her name back then was Edythe Walker; Evelyn is a pseudonym she uses for the phony psychic routine. And you'll love this: Evelyn means 'bird,' and Edythe means 'spoils of war,' or 'striving for wealth.' And boy, has *she* moved right on up. She's been married to a doctor—Frederick Trilby—for about ten years. He fancies himself quite the sophisticate and *bon vivant*, but I talked to a lot of nurses, and—"

"How'd you manage that?"

"Bought myself a white uniform and ate in the cafeteria—"

"Slick," he chuckled. "That's my girl."

"His nickname is 'Bellybutton Trilby' because when he operates on the society ladies he goes in that way to minimize the scar—but these days it actually refers to a mistake he made—"

"Bet it was a doozy."

"Yeah, he took out a woman's appendix—except there was nothing wrong with it. She was pregnant."

"Jesus." I heard his feet come off the desktop and hit the floor and the sound of his pen scratching across paper. Anything to do with babies, Houdini was immediately plugged in.

"Well, he might have *thought* he was God, but I guess he knows better now."

"Maybe not," Houdini said. "I heard *he* was the one who got in touch with Doyle regarding Madame Evelyn's newfound talent for talking to the spirits."

"Yep. And from what I gather, every few weeks she comes up with a spanking brand-new effect. She started small with table-tipping, and the usual clatter-and-tap, but now she's honed in on bigger and brighter and bolder phenomena."

"A pipeline to the angels, maybe?"

I snickered. "Nah, she has a spirit control."

"Don't tell me—let me guess. A Nipmuc maiden, or maybe a Pequot warrior?"

"Close. Her dead brother, Benjamin."

He gave a low whistle. "What else?"

"She does the paranormal shtick in the nude or wearing a flimsy see-through negligee. Recently Benjamin made her breast glow—as if spirit lights illuminated it. I guess she was naked that time—or maybe flashing them: opening and closing her robe."

"Yeah, a debutante slumming as a hoochie-coochie girl. That must've given 'em a thrill."

"Wicked," I teased. "She can also manifest ectoplasm—and guess where it emanates from—aside from the ... er, more public orifices, that is?"

"Christ. Tambourines, table-rapping, ectoplasm ... what was it Huxley said? Oh yeah. 'Spiritualism gives us the best reason in the world not to commit suicide. Better to be a chimney sweep living in a hovel, than to be called back to spout twaddle and perform like a circus dog—for some medium who's getting twenty bucks a session.'"

"The thing is, she doesn't charge a dime."

"So what's her angle?"

"Hobnobbing with Back Bay society and Boston Brahmins. She's a star attraction. And I bet dollars to donuts when you go in, you'll be sitting at the place of honor—on Madame Evelyn's sacred left—and don't be surprised if she shoves your hand between her legs when the spirits start up. Lots of extras with the hijinks."

"Hussy."

"Huh? Right, of course she is—"

He laughed. "No, I meant you. Shameful what an unmarried girl will say over the phone these days."

Then, I laughed, too.

Secretly, though, I was worried and very glad he'd be in Boston with *me* in just a week or two.

"HOW'D IT go?" I asked when he came to my room a little after midnight. Harry was staying at the stately old Copley Plaza, but he was there with Orson Munn, the publisher of *Scientific American*, the magazine that had offered a hefty cash-money prize to anyone who could be proved to be genuinely psychic. Houdini had tucked me into a small, quaint hotel not far from a trolley line.

He sat down in a flowered armchair and switched off the reading light alongside it. "Munn told me the most unbelievable rumor on the train up here," he said. "Do you know that people are saying Evelyn's husband surgically enlarged her vagina—so that she'd have more room to hide gimmicks?"

I blushed. "What an awful thought."

"It's disgusting, all right."

"Do you think it's true?"

"Leona, you would not believe what is going on in that séance parlor...."

I KNEW about Harry and his dalliances—with the wife of the famous writer, Charmian London; with the famous-in-her-own-right Gloria Swanson; with the Bay Area restaurant owner, Hattie Mooser; with another Martinka's alum, Daisy White. I knew about all of them. I knew he'd never leave Bess—and that was fine with me; I liked to think of myself as his soul mate, above petty rivalry. And up 'til now, I thought the way for us had been finally cleared. Who was this goddamn bitch, Evelyn, to come out of nowhere and seduce my Houdini? A lying, scheming slut, Sir Arthur's pet—which was a laugh since there never breathed a more chauvinistic soul. He was even against women's right to vote.

Worse, I knew he and Evelyn and dear Freddie were all anti-Semitic. Word had come back to me that her spirit control had made up a little singsong ditty early in July: "Harry Houdini, he sure is a Sheeny," it began. I thought it was disgusting. And most incredible to me of all, my sources informed me that Doyle himself was bigoted, too.

Harry had taught me information could be bought. So, just like the phony mediums, I bribed a maid and she read Trilby's correspondence—she even copied it out for me in clear, round Palmer method script onto sheets of Evelyn's rose-water-scented notepaper. The good doctor had written to Doyle that it was a shame that Houdini, "the low-minded Jew, had any claim even on the *word* American."

It sure didn't take any goddamn Sherlock Holmes to deduce that Trilby—a great pal of Doyle's—figured they were of the same mind-set. Not only was he writing letters, he was also sending His Lordship the detailed minutes of each séance. Would he allow that hideous epithet to go uncensored or without comment if he thought just seeing it on the page would offend Sir Arthur? Of course not. Doyle tempered his own public writing, but the prejudice leaped from between the lines; he found that Houdini's ways seemed "strange to our colder Western blood. There are many things in him as Oriental as there were in our own Disraeli." Another Jew by birth. *Speak for yourself, Doyle*, I thought.

"LEONA," Harry said, "I caught Evelyn out in spades. She's a total fraud...."

He went on, but I had a hard time concentrating. It didn't matter that I'd already told him about her sex games. My stomach was knotted with the fear that speaking those things aloud brought them to life. And then, all I could think about was Evelyn nude under her silk robe, tugging Houdini's hand, pulling it firmly, 'til his fingers were gliding up the wetness of her smooth inner thighs ... 'til they reached the tangle of glossy, reddish curls and she guided them—hungrily, wantonly—to the secret place inside her.

WE WERE back at the Blue Moon Café; I'd begun to think of it as Emory's place. It was blustery that night, and every time a patron left or entered, cold wind sheared through the cigarette haze. In my mind's eye, I was directing the arctic blasts and chuckled to see this overweight man or that too-scantily dressed girl shiver.

"I want to ask you something, Leona."

"I want to ask you something, Emory," I giggled.

"Seriously...."

"No, seriously...."

He sighed impatiently, then pressed on. "Did Houdini rig Evelyn's séances?"

"What, the stuff in the wooden box and the bell?" Houdini had detected Evelyn surreptitiously sliding her foot forward to press a bell to make it ring. After he told the *Scientific American* investigating committee, one of the members (who would have done anything for the sultry medium) betrayed his confidence and went racing back to tell Freddie and Evelyn. The next night, a tiny pencil eraser was found clipped under the board and the Trilbys—along with Evelyn's spirit guide, Benjamin—accused Houdini of planting it. Ditto, a folding ruler hidden in the wooden box Houdini constructed to keep Evelyn's hands and feet where they belonged.

"Yeah. That and other effects...."

"No, he didn't. And I know that for a fact."

Emory nodded. "I wondered."

"My turn. I wonder why this dump would care about Houdini's birthday enough to let you stage your own show."

"Huh?"

"It's not Halloween—it's not like ninety percent of the population even *knows* his birthday—so why would the management agree to a full night of magic?" I said. "Two nights, actually."

He blew out a puff of smoke and shrugged. "I asked, they said okay. They didn't care too much about the dates, so I suggested—"

"And your performance is gonna be a bigger draw than a dance band on a Saturday night? They'll sell more drinks when?"

He blushed.

"I mean the band plays, anyone can order beer and cocktails anytime—but you're up there, and the waiters are stuck behind the bar except during the applause."

"So what?"

"So, I think you're full of crap. I'm just not sure why you're spewing it."

"And I think you're as crazy as everyone told me you were."

I glared.

"Look at you, in here night after night, dressed like some Bowery palm reader, carrying a handbag filled with crumpled newspaper and Cracker Jack prizes and cardboard 'magic tricks' cut off the backs of cereal boxes! I only felt sorry for you—"

But I was already gone, pushing the brass handle on the wood and glass door. "Did you hear that, Harry?" I whispered, my heels clicking on the pavement. "Did you hear what he said?"

I WAS in the old library at 278 when the sconces came to life.

The electricity had been shut off—oh, years ago, I guess, but someone had placed thick white candles in each of the sockets and now as I sat there, I turned slowly to see them lighting, one by one. The air seemed to shimmer, and I smelled ozone. I saw it ripple—not the way it does over hot pavement on a summer day—but the way picnic blankets undulate when you're spreading them in the breeze before laying them on soft sand, or the way a magician's cape unfurls when he twirls it from his shoulders and floats it over the stage. Yes, like a magician's cape, I thought. And through the ripple, now the room—as it was when Harry lived here—could be seen. There was the standing globe, the long table, the mirrors, the ranks and ranks of tiered shelves crammed with books. There were the leather club chairs, the lamps with the fringed shades ... underneath my feet, the reddish brown of the antique Aubusson carpet bordered with a black background and gold medallions.

I moved toward the French windows that faced the back garden, to the alcove where the trance table once stood, its ebony gleaming amid ivory and abalone inlays.

I sat down and rubbed a finger across it.

One of its secrets was the tiny peg—the center of a floweret—that the medium could secretly fit into the back of an ordinary-looking ring and use to tilt the table, then release when it was upright. I probed gently ... and there it was.

"All this for me, Harry?" I breathed. "It's a lovely gift ... this room. I'm glad you remembered my other birthday. Not just the special one, but this one too, today, because it makes me feel like a young girl again."

There was a low susurration, part sigh, part rustling; then I saw the girandoles on the mantel sway. Their prisms chimed, the candle flames reflected scattered tiny scraps of rainbow across the walls and up onto the coffered ceiling.

"There's more, you say?"

I laughed and clapped my hands, bounced to my feet and found myself nearly skipping from room to room. It was all there: the opulent carpets; the dull satin drapes and Flemish paintings; the elegant teak dining room; the tidy kitchen with its painted wood table and towering cupboards; the foyer lined with potted ferns on marble pedestals and the ornate mirrored hall stand; the billiard room; the bedrooms—even the secret passageways behind book shelves and false-backed wardrobes. Up in the attic, under the eaves, Harry's mahogany desktop gushed piles of books and stacks of cascading papers. His chair spun slowly—as if he'd just gotten up to check a reference or gone down to the kitchen for a snack.

Even all the way up here, I heard the grandfather clock strike two.

"I'm sleepy, Harry," I murmured. The hidden door to a staircase was ajar. "You're right, it's quicker that way," I said, yawning. The tiny landing opened alongside the library fireplace and, a second later, I was lying back on a striped satin sofa tugging an afghan with pale blue fringe up to my shoulders. It was so nice to think of dreaming here— and better still, of waking in the born-again house.

IN MY DREAM, 278 was not only empty and forlorn, so that I wasn't comfortably warm and cozy on the down pillows of the sofa, I was lying on the chill concrete in the cellar with nothing to cover me except a drift of old leaves that'd been swept into a corner and never disposed of in the long-unused furnace. Upstairs, I could hear movement—footsteps and voices and laughter. "They've got a fire going up there," I whispered to myself, "why should I lie here in the damp?" But I hesitated ... a dark vibration passed through me and I realized, in part, I was afraid to climb the stairs, afraid of what I'd find and what I'd see.

"But you've got to," Emory exhorted me. "It's time you knew—the rest of us have been aware for decades. It's time for you to look in the mirror and take off the blindfold, Leona."

I laughed. "Emory, if you were anything better than a third-rate magician, you'd know that seeing through a blindfold is pure child's play. A kindergarten trick. There are sightlines to be found under layers and layers of cloth—even with five men holding their fingers over your eyes."

He gave a thin smile. "Oh yes, I know. Even about the reversible ones that seem legit to the audience—but gimmicked or straight—it's time for you to see everything clearly."

He pulled me up onto my feet, then gave me a hard shove toward the stairs. "Go on," he said. His hands pushed again when I hung back. "I'm right behind you. Move."

I was expecting to see the kitchen's green linoleum, but the door opened out from under the stairs in the front hall.

"This isn't 278!"

"Who said it was? We're more than two hundred miles from New York."

I did a quick mental calculation. "Boston!" Evelyn was sometimes called "The Red-Headed Witch of Myrtle Street," and I wondered if she'd gained the powers she coveted during her lifetime and transported me there. "I remember ... there's a park—with ... with a playground for children—down the block." My stomach roiled with uneasiness.

It was dark in the entryway—except for a single, amber flame-shaped bulb held aloft by a cast-bronze cherub mounted on the newel post of the stairs leading up. Its infantine body was naked, its babyish mouth smiled secretively, and I felt the thing leering at me.

"Where are we going?"

"You know, Leona: fifth floor, the top of the house ... the séance room."

IT WAS like viewing a film being shown out of sequence: snippets of time kaleidoscoped and fracturing, then becoming whole, then disintegrating again. But all of them were there with Evelyn—flickering in the gloom—adoring faces gathered round her, worshipping the shadow queen. But it was more than just seeing. From the time before talkies had been invented, I heard their voices. I could smell the wax Sir Arthur used on his mustache; his wife had recently discovered mediumistic talent and now she channeled an entity named Pheneas. Lady Doyle's hand drummed three times then moved like an automaton's, the pen she held violently etching paper with a sound like the claws of a trapped animal scrabbling for freedom; I saw Arthur Ford, black hair smoothed and sparkling with Brilliantine, demonstrating the trance state, mouthing the words he claimed emanated from *his* spirit control; I tasted port wine from Fred Trilby's glass, smelled the pungent chlorine in Dakin's solution from the operating room and the formaldehyde of the hospital morgue; I saw a baby's flaccid hand the medium claimed was ectoplasm emanating from the cleft between her thighs; I felt the impassioned fingers of the *Scientific American* committee men grazing Evelyn's hot skin, and I smelled her sex mingling with patchouli and gardenia; I watched Emory tutoring her as gold coins and pocket watches rattled out of thin air onto the séance table, birds materialized and flew about the room, blood streamed from her eyes, then finally she slumped to the floor at the same time her etheric body—pale and translucent—rose toward the ceiling and abruptly disappeared.

Three doves circled round and round in frenzy then lit on the top edge of what Evelyn, like other mediums of the day, called her cabinet—a place to gather psychic strength that was really nothing more than an ordinary three-fold screen covered in plain muslin cloth. The birds huddled, terrified, shifting uneasily against one another and softly cooing—until their faint cries became the whimpering of children.

"What has she done to them? She's trapped their souls!" I screamed. I ran at her, her long body still collapsed onto the floor, but Emory held me back.

"Nothing, Leona. She's done nothing—do you call a baby's soul trapped when it's in the womb?"

It was then I saw the gentle swell of her abdomen under the flimsy silk.

"WHO'S the father, Emory? And if you say it's Harry, I'm going to slap your face."

"All of them—not the way you think—but psychically. Their energies created this child and Benjamin breathed life into it from the other realm."

"That is blasphemy. An abomination. And I don't believe it."

"Blasphemy? Don't be ridiculous—you know that after the Great War there was a huge revival in Spiritualism," he said. "Millions of young men were blown to bits on the battlefields, millions more—including women and children and old people—died of malnutrition and diseases—"

"My father," I whispered.

"What—"

"My father died in 1918 from the flu. He—he wasn't even forty. And my sister—she was seventeen..."

"And those were *easy* deaths, Leona—compared to what soldiers suffered, compared to the anguish of mothers mentally reliving the torment of their sons' last moments, mothers whose boys went down in clouds of poison mustard gas, lay hacked apart by machine guns and bayonets and mortars. Those deaths were easy compared to the agonies of all those uncles and fathers and sons and brothers who died alone screaming in the frozen mud of the trenches, blasted to blood and bone."

I saw how it could be done ... how it would happen and what they planned for Harry.

"That's right. Men like Sir Arthur—important men whose every word the bereaved hang on—men and women who lost their sons. They *believe*. So much so, that even years later our numbers are still growing. And when the world learns about this? In less time than you can whisper *mirabile dictu*—wonderful to tell—there will be more Spiritualists than Christians."

I FELT caught up in a kind of peculiar half-waking, half-sleeping state—what that Dutch shrink Van Eeden, back in 1913 (at least according to my doctors) called lucid dreaming, or something very close to it. Somehow, I guessed, Emory magicked time into a Mobius strip—as pliable as the thinnest tissue paper—so it could bend and twist and roll back on itself....

I saw years of overlapping séances: Evelyn's first tentative foray into the recesses of her psyche; her circle of admirers gathered months later when Benjamin manifested his tame crow, Pluto, flapping madly and croaking doom for Houdini; Houdini himself, shrewdly honing in on Evelyn as the investigating committee locked her in the wooden box, her head protruding, her arms thrust through portholes at each side and held tightly by Harry and publisher Orson Munn to forestall her chicanery. I watched Dr. Bellybutton Trilby sneak a carpenter's folding ruler beneath the cushion at Evelyn's feet inside the box before the committee closed the metal hasps—so that during the dark séance she'd have no trouble making the bell chime. I saw Houdini, livid with anger, and heard him shout: "I know *exactly* how she rang that bell, and I'll show you how she did it right now! This minute!" I saw the early beginnings of the unholy alliance among Conan Doyle and Arthur Ford and Emory; their feigned public upset at the magician's death; their selfish plan to trick Beatrice, steal Houdini's secret code, and turn his crusade against fakery into the ultimate triumph for Spiritualism. Their chortling laughs over how the newspapers would have a global field day: *Famed Skeptic and Debunker Houdini Returns from the Dead! Tells Bess, the Afterlife is Real! From the Other Side Houdini Begs his Wife to Spread the Word. Magician who Testified for Congress that Mediums are Phonies Back from the Grave!*

Over and over, again and again—in rapid sequence—I saw the octagon of the séance table, the eager faces of the sitters charged with sexual energy and alternately gleaming by red lamplight, then submerged in total blackness.

It was dizzying. Almost nauseating. The constant strobe effect created a kind of mental remove, the sense of peering through a veil that reminded me of stage setting and watching backlit actors perform behind painted cheesecloth scrim—the same kind of translucent curtain directors use and abuse on Broadway, especially when they want to evoke fantasy or otherworldliness or dream.

"Not a scrim, Leona," Emory said. "A mirror. You know all about watching in mirrors, don't you?" His voice had a nasty, insinuating edge, and I turned to look at him. He was the dissolute sneering Barrymore now, mustache curving downward and counterpointing the heavy lower lip.

"Mirrors? I...." I was suddenly numb with confusion, as if I'd been wrapped in cotton batting—or worse, rolled in thick linen sheets doused in hot water—just like they used to bind Harry for escape challenges. Did he mean crystal instead of mirror? Sometimes we used mirrors when Harry and I performed the girl in the crystal ball trick— and with or without refracted light or swirling haze, there was always distortion. The image in the crystal was *always* skewed, I thought. Off-kilter. I was trying to ferret out his meaning, hesitating, passive— because I saw his anger and contempt mounting, and I couldn't grasp his implication. But in large part, that was because my head had started to throb and I felt a claustrophobe's sense of suffocation. I tried to take a deep breath—even pressed the flat of my hand against my diaphragm—but it was impossible. The sense of constriction and isolation and fear weighed me down completely. I remembered what Harry said when he talked about all the variations of his burial stunts— shackled underground, manacled in caskets on trestles, submerged in a coffin under water—but this time I couldn't relax. I couldn't breathe.

"HEARING his brags definitely spiked my guns," Houdini told the scribbling reporter. Harry stood, clad in brown swimming trunks, before a by-invitation-only crowd on the moist aqua tiles alongside the pool at the Shelton Hotel in New York.

Egyptian fakir Rahman Bey had been getting a lot of press—not to mention backing by notables in the scientific community—for claiming remarkable powers: hypnotizing animals, forcing steel pins through his

47

cheeks, but most importantly, because he could put himself into a cataleptic trance and be buried alive. Houdini caught his act at the Selwyn in the late spring of 1926 and watched as the young man was nailed up in an airtight wooden coffin for eight minutes. He was irritated as all hell because he'd already exposed these tricksters' gambits in his 1920 book, *Miracle Mongers and Their Methods*.

He was fifty-two, he explained, and he'd spent three weeks dieting and getting himself in top-notch shape. He intended to go the conjuror a *lot* more than one better. The Boyertown Casket Company had built Harry an airtight galvanized iron coffin, and now it floated in one corner of the pool in readiness as he spoke to the press. Physicians estimated the available air inside the box would last a man—at most— three or four minutes. It would take tinsmiths *eight* minutes just to solder the lid once Houdini was inside.

"I'm gonna lie down inside that coffin; it's gonna be sealed. Then my assistants are gonna hold it down under the water, and I'm not coming up for *one solid hour*," he said. "And I guarantee I'm not going into any phony 'cataleptic trance' to do it."

THE TEMPERATURE inside the iron box had risen to 99 degrees, and he was deathly white and dripping with sweat when he emerged, but the official time on the clock read: one hour, thirty-one minutes.

Houdini was thrilled over the *Times'* huge headlines, but he was more concerned about passing on what he'd learned to government officials and medical personnel who dealt with trapped miners and avalanche victims. He explained his techniques so that *lives* might be saved.

His peers assumed it was a stunt, but he wrote to other magician friends the box was genuine: "There is no invention to it, there is no trick, there is no fake; you simply lie down in a coffin and breathe quietly."

Mirrors. I clearly recalled what Houdini had told me about what the press deemed "The Shelton Pool Miracle," but my mind seemed to run on one track—a mental tic replayed again and again: He went into the galvanized iron box wearing only a bathing suit and an oversized watch with a radium dial. There were two wires—one connected to a signal bell in case of emergency, the other to a battery-operated telephone an assistant monitored. The watch and the wires ... and that was all. Watch, swimsuit, and wires. No fakery, no smoke, no mirrors—so why did I relate a mirror to his escape?

I could clearly visualize the large rectangle of a slanted mirror just above his face. I shook my head—that was wrong—over his face there'd been a glass porthole. What would be the point of a mirror? And the mirror I kept visualizing wasn't flat, wasn't set into the lid— and the only angled mirrors I associated with the sort of long tubular contrivance the Boyertown Casket Company came up with were ... were attached to medical devices for sick *children*....

DESPITE what Emory said about my father's and sister's "easy deaths," I suffered a sense of tremendous loss. I think Houdini understood that. When, in 1913, his beloved mother, Cecilia, died—a woman he adored so much he surprised her with a gown once owned by Queen Victoria—he wrote afterward about losing the will to live.

Equilibrium and desire and ambition shattered ... no one talks about the personal loss after trauma. For me, time literally changed. Not just before or after those deaths—a kind of demarcation that existed in my mind, but *all* time after. I no longer had the ability to pinpoint events and their dates from 1918 on—I merely guessed.

So you'll understand that I believe (but I'm speculating) that it was a Saturday morning in autumn 1921 when Houdini and I headed north to nearby Westchester County. Houdini especially loved performing magic for kids—and even more so if they'd been hospitalized. He liked to be the bright spot—even for an hour or two—in those little lives that were circumscribed by dread and pain and loneliness. He did the flashy miniaturized show by himself, and I stood around with the nurses and watched the small miracle unfold: For eighty, ninety, maybe one hundred minutes—he produced stuffed rabbits out of silk top hats for the children, towering bouquets of red roses from stainless steel ice-water pitchers for the staff, and boxes of confetti and cookies for everyone—illness and death itself fled forgotten; laughter and excitement held sway.

I was carrying a small box of equipment to set in the backseat of his big Pierce Arrow when I heard him call my name. He'd been strolling more leisurely across the lawn with the charge nurse. He caught up to me. "Miss Giddens just told me that her sister—a Franciscan nun—works at a hospital called St. Agnes. It's not far at all—"

"White Plains can't be more than seven or eight miles," she said.

49

"And with the parkway, you'd be able to zip right back to the city afterward ... should I call her and say you want to visit the children?"

"What do you think, Leona?" He was practically dancing with enthusiasm, toes twinkling on the bluestone gravel of the driveway. "Couple hours—tops."

"Sure—why not?" I smiled. I could never refuse Harry anything.

I CAN'T really remember why I didn't watch Houdini's brief performance in the children's ward at St. Agnes. I seem to remember leaving the long room with its neat rows of beds (a few minutes after he started the show) in order to search for a ladies' room. I recall leaving—I don't remember why I didn't go back when, confused in the maze of the hospital corridors, the visitors' bathroom eluded me.... And I don't remember fleeing the old brick building in a panic or the hours I spent cowering in the tiny cave-like stone grotto on the grounds, praying and whimpering in front of a polychrome statue of the Virgin, dazed and terror-stricken, kneeling in a cold puddle of my own urine ... until Harry finally found me.

WHAT I do remember is the sound of my heels clicking against the gleaming, waxed wooden floors through hallway after hallway, and hurriedly pushing open a frosted-glass-windowed door in search of a staff member who might direct me to the nearest toilet where I could relieve my throbbing bladder.

The chalky-white room had been darkened—its tall windows leaked a few thin streaks of daylight around the heavy green shades that were so popular back then.

At first, I thought I'd wandered into one of the labs on account of the faint, constant hum of machinery. My eyes adjusted to the gloom, and I saw there were ranks and ranks of tubelike metal cylinders lying horizontally on bright steel gurneys. The large, bullet-shaped containers stretched from wall to wall, humped in rows like a schematic of army barracks, all of them the same ugly, antiseptic beige—the gleamless, worn color of an old woman's teeth.

I drifted further inside, some part of me estimating their number—thirty, forty, perhaps as many as fifty, inside that dim, cavernous space. Except for that rhythmic sound—a kind of slow wheezing—the room was a study in silence.

Then, two things happened simultaneously or nearly so: First, a door opened at the far end—banged hard enough to hit the wall and rattle its glass pane. I was expecting a reprimand from some curmudgeonly doctor of research for disturbing the peace and sterility of what I took to be experiments in progress, and I smiled nervously—though I wasn't sure the figure could see it through the gloom from sixty or seventy feet away.

"Didn't you see the sign?" a harsh woman's voice boomed from behind a cotton mask. I kept approaching, and now I saw she also wore a white uniform. A nurse.

"Sign? I was looking for the—"

"Sign! The orange sign! On the door! This ward is off-limits—quarantined!"

The second event came into play, and I noticed each of the six-foot-long cylinders held a large rectangular mirror angled just above a sort of porthole—an opening, I realized too sluggishly, that allowed the patient's head to protrude where it lay on a white pillow. And the mirrors were in place ... because they allowed the only type of window into the world these stricken ones could have—with the seemingly towering upright frontage of those ... those iron lungs. The tubes were *iron lungs*.

My chest heaved. I felt such terrible sadness thinking of their profound isolation. No one to touch or hold them ... no hand to take one of theirs. Only the invisible ministrations of a masked nurse—opening a hinged side panel they couldn't even lift their heads to see—to administer an injection, or tug the white bedsheets flat, or quickly and efficiently sponge their pallid flesh. The fear, the loneliness, the desolation. I shook my head, woozy with complete understanding. The goddamn slanted mirrors were the *only* form of human contact these poor enfeebled wraiths *could* have before most of them succumbed to paralysis, or to death.

The interplay of those two events produced a third shock: Worse than the insidious sound of mechanical breathing, worse even than the terrible truth of those mirrors and the sense of near-complete isolation they conveyed, was a thought—no, a certainty, a *conviction*—that made me stagger. The real but awful knowledge that raced through me with the speed of a lightning bolt, went bone-deep, was a scream inside my head: *Polio!*

There was absolutely not a single shred of doubt in my mind that I was going to contract the disease and be locked inside an iron lung with nothing but that ragged sound and the horror of facing death completely bereft ... and utterly alone.

IN TERROR, I raced outside and stumbled into the limestone grotto near the entrance of St. Agnes. Some dim part of me had registered the weathered verdigris plaque over the entry:

SANCTA MATER
ORA PRO NOBIS

Blessed Mother, pray for us.

Of course, to Catholics, it also meant, Holy Mother, *intercede* for us.

So, I knelt at the same time I yanked faded dollars and spilled silver coins out of my pocketbook, stuffing the currency into a tiny square iron box, took thin wax spills from the ledge and lit votive candle after candle, my mind blanked with fear and panic. Please, *please*, I begged. *Oh, please,* I gabbled, unaware of even whether I spoke aloud or inwardly, oblivious to both the cold, unforgiving marble beneath my knees and to the wet patch of my own body waste ... oblivious 'til Harry found me still kneeling, but amid a welter of broken red glass and congealing white wax and splintered wooden crutches I'd pulled—and smashed in a perfect fury—from the grotto's stony throat.

OBSESSION

The dream-Emory was gone. But my memories of the time after we went to St. Agnes Hospital swirled and seethed even as I lay on the damp cellar floor in 278, semilucid and completely still—as still as any polio victim half-swooning in her iron lung.

Was it a premonition that bright autumn day? Or was it just a guess composed of nine-tenths fear and one-tenth awareness that, as a young person who traveled a great deal, my chances for exposure were hugely magnified?

You have to remember, I reminded myself, how little was known about the disease back then—Salk's vaccine, first tested four years ago and finally available just last year in 1955, wasn't even a wild gleam in some scientist's eye. Back then, all they speculated was that *some* people were carriers—just like with diphtheria or typhoid. Sure, blame it on Typhoid Mary, Diphtheria Dottie, and Polio Polly, I chuckled to myself. But really, they weren't sure how it spread—fly-infested outhouses, tainted water, contaminated milk, dirty swimming pools? Nobody knew for sure—except that it was mostly a disease of children and young adults and it spread more fiercely in summer and autumn. There was no penicillin either—if you got a disease like polio, the best they could do was give what they called "convalescent serum"—blood from someone who'd recovered. The other treatments consisted of medical regimens on a par with the type of care practiced in the 18th century—keeping the patient calm, completely immobile, and lowering fever with quinine and sponge baths.

I remembered, too, how one night, the words I heard one doctor whisper kept me awake a long time: differential diagnosis.

It meant—when you first began to exhibit typical symptoms like fever and malaise and headache, and before they could be sure what was wrong—guesswork about the nature of your disease. With polio, the list was pretty short: meningitis, encephalitis, or, very occasionally, hysteria—at least until paralysis set in. Then, unless it *was* hysteria, they could be very goddamn sure.

HARRY broke the news to me.

"NO, DON'T try to talk," a voice said quietly. I felt fingers lightly smooth my hair away from my temples and remember thinking absurdly, I was so sweaty and damp and I couldn't remember the last time I'd washed it, and it probably smelled as bad or worse than the malodorous stench that passed for air around me, but the fingertips felt cool and soothing.

The room was cast in semidarkness and my eyelids were heavy, sluggish. Still, I recognized the face floating in front of me and grinned: I was having a hallucination, because here was Houdini—from chin to eyebrows—hovering a mere six inches above the tip of my nose. Clearly impossible in real life, and he'd never stoop to a cheap trick like the ones fake mediums used.

"It's good to see you smile," he said. "You had us all scared out of our wits, kiddo, keeling over like that on the train to Albany."

It was getting hard to think. "I—"

I felt his index finger rest delicately against my lips, as if to hush me, but hadn't seen his hand flash up. "Doctor says you've got to rest—and rest completely."

"Wh—?"

"An ambulance brought you here. Hospital for now, and we'll see what's what later." There was a hitch in his voice, and I thought I saw a tear high on his cheek, but when I went to lift my hand to brush it away, my fingers seemed faraway and dead.

"No more tonight," Harry whispered. "Later." He touched me lightly, gently trailing the sensitive skin from just beneath my earlobe and downward. "Tomorrow, okay?"

Then he was gone, and the room was very quiet except for a prolonged in-and-out whooshing sound that surrounded me like a caress—like the soft knowing fingertips that glided through my hair and traced compassion along my cheek—until I dropped into the womb of sleep.

I BELIEVE it was the next day—when, as he'd promised, Harry visited me for the second time—that I began mentally treading the slow loop of the knowledge I'd been stricken with polio.

"Is she the high-strung sort, Mr. Houdini?" a low voice asked.

"High-strung? Well, no ... I mean, she's very artistic, she's one of my assistants on stage, you know, and all the box jumpers—the girls—and my wife, too—they're very painstaking—perfectionists and all—"

"The reason I ask is, because once in a while, young girls like Leona, well, they're not pretending; they really do believe they *are* sick, but it turns out their minds *create* the symptoms. It's something that alienists—mental doctors—are just beginning to learn about and—"

"Excuse me, Doctor ... Doctor Werther? I think you told me earlier your name was Doctor Werther?"

"Werner."

"Pardon me. Dr. Werner. You're in general practice—"

"Post-grad now and I have a great deal of training in mental disease—"

"I don't doubt your skills in the least," I heard Harry say. "But Leona's temperature, when she fell sick on the train, was 104. That doesn't sound like hysteria to me—that sounds like a very sick girl. Dr. Thompson—my personal physician from Columbia Presbyterian in New York City—he told me—" And here his voice dropped to a whisper, "*he's* sure it's polio."

AT TIMES, my mind felt brittle with the fever—as if it were about to overheat like unglazed pottery left too long in a kiln then begin to crumble. I was aware of the mechanical push-pull action of the air pulsating around inside the tank, which forced my chest to rise and fall. I'd been wrong that day back at St. Agnes when I thought the motors had a soothing rhythm. It was a terrible noise that sounded ragged to me now, and with each squeeze and release I felt more anxious, more powerless ... as if I were being invaded.

Harry had snagged a white metal chair and sat alongside the iron lung with me for a long time—even when the ward nurse (a statuesque redhead) came to snap open the side portholes and bathe me with less tenderness than a two-year-old dunking a rubber dolly into a puddle.

"No need for you to leave, Mr. Houdini," she told him. I heard the low excitement in her voice—a cat's purr, submissive and seductive in the face of his celebrity.

"Well—"

"She's completely concealed inside the apparatus—all very proper and modest."

I could barely hear the swish of the sponge in the enamel basin; I was more aware of the unpleasant feel of tepid water dribbling on my skin.

"No, don't try to help," she suddenly snapped at me. I wasn't aware I'd stirred or even flinched. It was all so far away and disconnected, I might have been on the moon.

"*We must never let the patient move their affected muscle*s," she told Harry. Her voice was saccharine—for his sake—but I could tell she was speaking by rote. "At this stage, when there's nothing that can be done. It's harder on the family than the patient," she said.

The porthole clicked shut and she began to walk away.

I looked up at him and our eyes met. Our fingertips had touched secretly on stage a thousand times, in the perfection of his magician's art, in the creation of spectacle and of illusion. He held so much power, so much strength.

God, I wished I could hold his hand.

THE PASSING of time was dimmed in the semidarkened room, or perhaps I dozed. But a few minutes or an hour later—it doesn't matter—I was aware that Houdini, the greatest living escape artist and conjuror, was still at my side, patiently keeping vigil.

"Can't you help me?"

"Help you?" he repeated.

"Yes. Make me well. You—" I wheezed.

His face went deep scarlet and I saw his hand flash up, felt the tips of the first two fingers delicately press my lips. "Ssh ... please don't talk." He swallowed. "I think I know what you mean, Leona," his voice wavered, "because this has happened twice before." He pulled his chair closer, leaning forward so that his broad chest was resting lightly against the top of my head. His face swam nearer and larger in the slanted mirror, his blue eyes darkened with sorrow.

"When my mother died in 1913, everyone knew how devastated I was. There was a light gone from my life that could never gleam—or even flicker—again. Everyone knew. But it was Jim Collins—my assistant—the man who helped create all my secrets and built my tricks and illusions, who came to me and said, 'Houdini, can't you bring her back?'" He paused. "He was dead serious, Leona, and it *stunned* me. If there was anyone in the world who'd understand I am not a god, that I have no occult powers, it was Jim." He gently smoothed the hair from my forehead. "But then...." He cleared his throat, and I saw his eyes were already misting. "In February 1917, I was in Boston performing; and so was Sarah Bernhardt. I'd done her a little favor just before that—"

I shook my head. It was no "little favor"; it had been reported in newspapers worldwide. Houdini thought the legendary French actress was brilliant and wrote about her prowess in his *Daily Mirror* column— but he was even more roused by her outspoken pleas for the human rights of Jews in Russia. Bernhardt had recently been given a special award in the form of a bronze statuette—unfortunately, she'd also received a bill for the same from the artist's wife. Bernhardt returned the two-foot-tall statue—and the bill. Houdini immediately took charge, paying the full amount and reclaiming the bronze to give it to Bernhardt. The press lapped it up.

"You're pretty young, so I'm not sure how much of this you know, but back in 1905, Bernhardt severely injured her leg while jumping from the parapet when she played *Tosca*. She was still on stage, still in the limelight, but her leg never really healed." He swallowed. "Gangrene set in and, the year before I saw her in Boston, they'd had to amputate. So, she was performing, but only with the aid of a wooden leg. Anyhow, she invited me to her hotel room and I did some close-up magic for her, and she really enjoyed it. The next day, she came to watch me escape from a straitjacket, hanging by my heels six stories up. Afterwards, we were riding in her car, and she suddenly startled me, saying, 'Houdini, you're a wonderful human being and you have these extraordinary powers. Please. Can't you restore my leg?'

"I was shocked, and I told her, 'Madame, truly, my powers are limited and you're asking me to do the impossible.'

"She leaned closer and took hold of my coat lapel and looked into my eyes. 'But Houdini, you *do* the impossible.'

"You're joking, aren't you?" I said.

"'*Mais non*, Houdini, *j'ai jamais été plus sérieux dans ma vie.*' But no, Houdini, I've never been more serious in my life—she was saying." He paused. "I felt so sad, so helpless...."

"Leona, you mean so much to me. I really hoped we," he faltered. "And now, now this terrible—terrible *affliction.*" He laid his palm against my cheek and, weakly, I turned my head to kiss it. "I'll do what I can, Lee—I promise you that—but I cannot promise to do the impossible ... it would disappoint *and* devastate us both."

I WAS thrilled he'd told me how much I meant to him and even more secretly pleased he'd called me Lee. No one else—except my father—had ever used it. In my heart, I knew it was an endearment, that he cherished me. I liked it even more because, of course, Houdini's name was really Ehrich, and now that *his* mother was gone, only Bess still sometimes called him Ehrie; Harry was actually the Americanized version of his childhood pet name.

But when he left that afternoon, I found myself recalling the previous autumn and the day at St. Agnes Hospital. After that unnerving flash of certitude, after that agonizing premonition and the fear and rage I expended in the holy grotto, I spent seven or eight long months convincing myself I'd gotten hysterical for nothing. Clearly, I told myself, I'd been dead wrong. I remember praying to my guardian angel night after night alone in my narrow bed, and hearing her comforting whisper in my mind, "See, Leona, not every suspicion—no matter how overwhelming or absolute it seems—is correct. Not everything we fear—*not every intuition that shakes us to our core*—comes to pass."

Part of me felt relieved by these gentle assurances as I drifted in the dark toward sleep; another more sentient part balked when that candied inner voice spoke up. Invariably, a sharp thrust, stabbing downward from gullet to stomach, made me jerk abruptly like a gunshot victim and reminded me in the most visceral terms that I was (rightly) terrified.

I think it was mid-May of 1922 when the weather turned unseasonably hot for the better part of a week. After the evening show, one of the stagehands armed sweat from his brow and desultorily suggested we ought to day-trip over to Staten Island on the ferry—maybe tote along a picnic lunch—and head for Woodland Beach. Naturally, the group of us who were enthused about this prospect invited Harry and Bess to come along—but Houdini declined: "I need to set up some little 'experiments' at 278 before Sir Arthur arrives tomorrow night," he said.

"I ought to skip the picnic and help you," I said.

"No, go on, Leona. Go enjoy yourself, you deserve a break. Just stop by in the morning and we'll go over the plans for all the effects, and then be back by seven, before Doyle gets there."

I REMEMBER the hot sun, the sparkling waves, and later in the afternoon—after the damage was already done, after I was both betrayed by another and, in turn, betrayed myself and Houdini—I watched the serried clouds massing and, eventually, graying the horizon, suddenly shedding huge, stinging drops, unaware the skies wept in anticipation for what was to come.

There were five or six of us that day, and I chummed with a prop girl—another Martinka's alum—named Malvina Parker. We sang Al Jolson's "Toot-Toot Tootsie, G' Bye," striding over the sand arm-in-arm toward a pair of adjoining cabanas to change out of our street clothes. "You know," I told her as we reached the cunning little white, wooden houses and I pulled open the creaking door, "this reminds me of my Italian grandmother—who lived up in the country around Tarrytown. She always called her outdoor toilet the 'back-haus' and, when I was a kid, I had trouble understanding her accent. I thought she was saying the 'because,' which made a weird sense to me—it was the 'because' *because you had to go;* and *that* sounded more ladylike than outhouse," I said, and Malvina laughed.

"Say, speaking of the 'because,' did you happen to see one on our way here?"

"There are bathrooms in all the hotels," I said, glancing away from the sea toward the boardwalk.

"Oh, Leona, I couldn't," she said. "You're not supposed to go into those places unless you're a guest."

"The Richmond is right there. Couldn't we just ask some friendly looking person sitting out on the veranda to—to escort us?"

She grabbed my arm. "There's got to be a loo in the public bath house. C'mon—we can come back to change." Perverse as it sounds, there was always something about those slightly worn but solid, huge, old wooden structures that smelled of ladies' talcum, creosote, sea salt, and whitewash that I had a distinct nostalgia for—they summoned up the rare summer excursions of my childhood to Coney Island. So, good-naturedly, I followed her (even waiting on line to use one of the rank chemical toilets tacked on to the monolith of the bath house). On our way back to the changing booths, a voice from the second floor porch of the Richmond called out to her: "Malvina! Miss Parker!"

We stopped short and turned to see a young man with glossy black hair waving.

Malvina shaded her eyes with a cupped palm. "Look, there's my friend, Arthur Ford," she said. "It's okay, Leona. He's not a masher. I know him."

THE NAME should have registered with me. In 1921, Ford had not only set himself up as a trance medium with a control named Fletcher, but established a Spiritualist church in New York. *It should have.* But lulled by the hot sun, his glib talk, and the halcyon setting, it didn't.

Ford insisted we have tea on the seaside verandah at the Richmond—and later, by the time I was already under his spell (caught by his fierce, gleaming eyes and his verbal caresses) that we leave the group to their own devices on the beach and spend a quiet, idyllic afternoon, just the three of us. Malvina was there. I saw nothing amiss, nothing untoward, nothing compromising. I should have recognized his name, but how could I know that Malvina was jealous of me, of my position in the troupe, of Harry's affection for me; like Bess in the years after Harry died, she was hopelessly in love with the clairvoyant scoundrel. She'd have done anything for him. She'd taken advantage of this impromptu outing to Staten Island, away from Houdini—had, in fact, arranged this "accidental meeting" and our severance from the rest of the troupe on the beach. As one of Harry's secretly disguised investigators of fake mediums, I should've guessed, but didn't, that Ford—sly as silk—was pumping *me* for information and already plotting the magician's downfall.

"YOUR FACE is flushed. Too much sun, Leona?" Harry teased.

I'm sure I blushed more deeply, thinking he'd read my thoughts, caught a glimpse of the inner glow still warming me after the postnoon frolic with Ford. I was still so fevered and overenthusiastic, I gushed: "I didn't go to the beach—Malvina introduced me to a friend of hers. He bought all three of us a picnic lunch they put up for guests at the Richmond, and then we all went to a wooded pond. He rented a canoe and helped me—us, I mean—gather water lilies. It was so peaceful ... just beautiful."

"And who is this knight-errant, this young Lochinvar?" He grinned.

"I'm not sure if he—that is Arthur—ever worked at Martinka's like Malvina—but that's where she met him."

"Arthur?"

"Yes, Arthur Ford. And he was positively floored when I mentioned that Conan Doyle was going to be at 278 this evening. I think he's written to Sir Arthur—as a fan, you know. And he's a great admirer of yours, too. He's been to your show—I don't know how many times."

A shadow crossed Houdini's face when I mentioned Ford's name, but he didn't elaborate—he merely inquired. "And you say he's a magician?"

"An amateur, probably." I shrugged. "But that's what Malvina said. And that he hung around Martinka's a lot—and at first I thought he might be a beau of hers—but...." I hesitated. "He paid a lot of attention to me, so I guess they're not a couple."

"What did he ask you? What did you tell him?" Houdini said.

We were cut off by the clangor of the door chime announcing Doyle's arrival, but I'd already begun to feel a little foolish. I loved Houdini by then, and it seemed callow on my part to fall sway to the oily flattery of a stranger—good looking or not.

Harry never brought it up again, but he knew exactly who Ford was, and I never found out if he guessed the depth of the medium's then-clandestine association with Sir Arthur.

IN 278, I was still trapped in the whirlpool of memories surrounding my long, terrible illness. During those first weeks caged inside the iron lung, I told myself I could never be *sure* if I'd gotten polio from visiting the stinking chemical toilets or from scooping handfuls of pond water as Arthur Ford paddled the canoe. I remembered how suavely—and seemingly hospitably—he fixed a plate from the huge picnic hamper for me, and how when I expressed delight in the pickled herring (which I'd never tasted before and he said he'd ordered specially) he kept urging more on me and without realizing it, I ate all of the appetizer myself. When the three small flasks of lemonade were gone, he urged me to quell my thirst—magnified by the heat and the salty fish—with pond water. He even shipped the paddle and filled one of the empty bottles for me several times as we drifted.

Once, years later, someone told me Ford was either a carrier or that he'd had a brief bout and recovered—which could have meant if he handled infected materials, then touched me—as he'd done, lightly smoothing my face and mouth, bringing my fingers to his lips to kiss—he'd given it to me.

Houdini had many other investigators—not just in New York, but across the country. But, except for Bess, there was no one closer, no one more privy to his methods and secrets. For a long time, while I was in the upstate hospital inside the iron lung, I was wracked with guilt. Orphaned and immature at twenty, I was already lonely, and I'd punished myself by creating a sense of abandonment and isolation I'd only half-glimpsed that brisk fall day at St. Agnes. The only time I felt peace—the satisfaction that comes from confidence—the only time I really felt *alive* was on stage. I'd betrayed Houdini; I'd betrayed myself and my feelings for him. Hardest of all to bear was the memory of the last evening I spent in a private room just off the polio ward at St. Peter's hospital in Albany, of the words Harry spoke to me, of the anguish we both felt.

"Company, Miss Derwatt," a night nurse announced.

I turned my head to see Houdini standing by the door, his hands held at waist height, his fingers nervously clutching the brim of a soft gray fedora.

This time, there was no banter, no attempts to jolly the patient. "I have to leave in a few hours to resume the tour. I don't want to go, but there are scheduled performances ... contracts," he said.

I closed my eyes. "Of course you have to go."

"Before I do, there's something I want—need, actually—to tell you." He took a deep breath. "I've been married to Bess a long time; I do love her; I could never leave her ... she depends on me."

I nodded. The whole troupe knew: Bess drank, she experimented with drugs, was ill—prostrate—often. "I think the things she does," I said, "are a way of avoiding emotional collapse ... the sadness and depression."

"I researched it ... doctors call it neurasthenia ... I think—well, it's maybe *one* of the things wrong ... but even if I could never marry you, Lee, until ... or *unless* something happened, I was in love with you. I'd even hoped," his voice sank, "that—I know it's impossible—but I even hoped we might have a child."

There was nothing to say, nothing I could say. Like many young women with polio, the disease had ravaged my body so completely I no longer menstruated.

I began to weep silently.

He stood alongside me a long time, wiping the brimming tears coursing down my face, the pads of his fingers gently and slowly blotting each. Then he did something I could never forget if I lived another century: He raised a fingertip and brought one shining drop to his lips and kissed it.

I understood it was our communion.

Then he leaned forward and his lips brushed my forehead.

Even if I recovered enough to live without the mechanical respirator, to walk—perhaps even to perform again—both of us knew the time for any physical union between us had passed—lost to the disease, lost in the waste of a damaged endocrine system, in the damped, nearly absent sexual fervor that would stay with me the rest of my life.

The inner pain, the guilt only mounted in the face of what Harry did next. He refused to accept what the redheaded nurse had told him—that nothing could be done. Instead, he arranged for a portable breathing machine and a different nurse and a car to take me back to New York. For several months, he paid for my stay at Columbia-Presbyterian Hospital, and for the expensive injections of convalescent serum made with antibodies from recovered polio victims. He and Bess brought me to live at 278. "You must never give up, Leona," he told me. Then he sought out special treatment in a warm-water pool to help me regain the use of my limbs. The thought of the therapeutic pool brought me full circle to my memories of Houdini's triumphant submersion in the iron box at the Shelton....

It was time, I knew, to discover the truth of my past—of years lost to mental fog and emotional shadows; the truth of what envious, greedy magicians and mediums—like Emory and Ford and their rabid Spiritualist coterie—had done to *him*.

INFESTATION

Emory's first solo gig was exactly one week away when I decided to go undercover to visit the Blue Moon Café. Back in the '20s, Houdini not only sent me and other investigators out to trap fake psychics, he sometimes wore disguises and went in for the kill himself. Once in Chicago, I believe, he caught a trumpet medium red-handed ... or maybe dirty-handed would be a more appropriate term, since as soon as the lights were doused, Houdini quickly opened a can of shoeblack he'd smuggled in and liberally coated the trumpet. The instant the thing began sailing around the room, Harry whipped out his flashlight and every sitter present was privy to the sight of the professed Spiritualist's hands and face smeared with Blackola, "the only shoe polish tin with a patented opening key." We had a good laugh over *that* little irony—and Harry taught me a lot about the art of concealment—that it didn't just depend on makeup and props—presentation was the real key. Undoubtedly, you know he was a master—especially if you've seen that famous photo of him dressed as an old man and waving a cane after he successfully orchestrated the arrest of still another phony clairvoyant.

It'd been years since I felt the belt of adrenaline that comes with spying. Sifting through the drift of my own small stock of photos, and recalling Houdini's techniques, I settled on the pretense of selling flowers—it would give me the opportunity to work the bar without being obvious. I bought three or four dozen white carnations, trimmed the stems an inch or so with a knife, then set them in a bucket filled with water and McCormick food coloring until the petals turned pale green. People, I knew, would be more inclined to focus on the wicker tray of flowers rather than on me—which would give me ample opportunity to pay attention to them, find one or two that were easy to sight-read, and—with a bit of subliminal suggestion or outright covert hypnosis on my part—likely to tell me what I wanted to know.

By nine o'clock, the West Side St. Patrick's Day crowd was in full party mode: swilling emerald beer and brown stout, tipsily forming spontaneous groups of three or four to croon popular Irish tunes like "It's a Long way to Tipperary"—with or without the band's accompaniment—ready to knock heads with any man who wouldn't declare that John L. Sullivan was the greatest boxer of all time; that Trinity was the best university anywhere in or out of Dublin; that the Liffey's Grand Canal was superior in every way to the piddling stream that ran through dreary ould Venice; and that, sure, even the holy Pontiff himself knew Guinness was the preferred ambrosia among the sainted in heaven—as well as a necessary and abiding comfort for the damned and miserable here on earth.

"A flower for the lady, or a nice buttonhole for yourself, sir, to celebrate the day?"

"One of each...."

"Oh, excellent," I said, handing over the long stem to a thirtyish woman then clipping the second smaller carnation. I took my time adding snippets of white ribbon and curling the ends with blunt scissors while I watched his face more closely.

"There, all set now, sir. Shall I pin it on for you?" He was nodding, but of course, my hands were already hovering in place. "And if I do say so, I think a man always looks his most dashing with a bit of God's natural finery on his lapel."

"What's your name?"

"Mary," I said.

"Mary, you're not from the ould sod, but you've the look of a Kilkenny lass—"

"You're not far wrong, sir; my mother was raised up on the coast of Wicklow," I laughed, "but isn't *everyone* Irish tonight?" He grinned, and quickly I said, "Do you come here often or are you part of the overflow from MacDoon's or Donegal's?"

"Every tavern in New York is an Irish pub tonight, Mary."

"We'll shake on that," I said, taking his hand and simultaneously tapping his wrist lightly with my left index finger—what's known as an induction handshake—a tiny, scarcely perceptible interruption in a standard cultural action that creates a sort of blank space in a person's thoughts and registers subliminally. A space a hypnotist could fill.

He'd bought the two carnations, told me his name was O'Keefe and that the woman sitting next to him, as I'd already picked up on, wasn't his date. I purposely hadn't asked him for the payment yet. I wanted information—if it could be had. "I was just wondering if you come here regular-like, because I heard that next week there's going to be a magician," I said.

"Magician! Svengali is more like it!"

"What do you mean?"

"I was here a few weeks ago, and him and his brother—though if it was his brother they were about as like as a hog and a rhino—got the whole kip here in an uproar. Mary, he stood at the mike, palaverin' and the next thing, everybody on the right side was wavin' at those on the left—thought they was seeing them off at the docks for a transatlantic sail!"

"And did you wave?"

"I was waved *at*. But for a second, Mary, on my mother's grave, I'd have sworn—that with the shouts and cheering and the heaps of pastel paper streamers unfurlin'—I'd have sworn I smelled the sea and heard the boat's big booming."

I'd seen Emory's magic tricks—the up-close work. With Ford or another box jumper, I expected he'd cobble together an escape, and based on what O'Keefe told me, that he was clearly going to work up a few clairvoyant numbers—altogether a satanic travesty of Harry's final shows.

A TILT of the head, a lilt in the voice—useful tricks both; I knew O'Keefe had seen me as a much younger woman. Like an actress playing a role, the best make-up one can don is the literal belief in being that character. Minutes after I departed the bar, he'd gather himself and wonder if he'd been talking to someone thirty-five with a girlish waist and bright fire in her eyes or a woman flying headlong toward sixty whose right foot dragged a bit when she was overtired or a little tipsy. But it wouldn't matter then. In the meantime, there was information to be gleaned.

"And you say he has a brother?" I asked. Years ago, Houdini had befriended a pair of celebrated magicians named Davenport, who were in fact siblings. They never claimed to be clairvoyants—but it hadn't stopped the Spiritualists from claiming *them* as virtuoso mediums who could manifest contact with the other side at each and every performance. Ira had even showed Harry their famous Davenport tie—which allowed him and William to slip their bonds and, ostensibly locked inside a heavy wooden cabinet, produce the ghostly sounds that titillated their audiences.

"At the end, they put on an act with mind reading and the like," he said. "As Fletcher and Fell—a kind of guide that comes through the Emory fellow when he falls into a trance. They could tell you all manner of things: what was in your pockets and where you lived or worked."

It was standard stuff, I knew—even if O'Keefe or the Blue Moon patrons didn't. Mind reading was easy because all that was necessary was an agreed upon code between the conspirators. So that if Fletcher called out (say), "I want you tell me what this is," the correct answer—given immediately by a blindfolded Emory as Fell—would be "Aspirin"; "Can you say what this is?" would elicit "Coin"; "I'd like to know this article, please," signified what was held up was a mechanical pencil. It was a routine that delighted—but the ESP gambit and its endless permutations had been around for decades. None of it was difficult—all of it was mere razzle-dazzle. More insidiously, as I was aware, information could be gleaned by parsing telephone directories or newspapers (and it would be even easier to look up impressive-sounding facts and figures in a bar that had regulars than it would be in a typical audience). The mediums could also pay spies to listen to conversations, to go through coats that were checked in a cloakroom for pay stubs, business cards, and love letters—then call out the "discoveries," knowing precisely who would respond to a query like, "I believe there's a gentleman here whose first initial is M, who resides in Chelsea, and who also works in banking." Operatives scoped out the obituaries, and the medium would then begin to transmit messages from M's dead grandmother, sister, uncle, brother—everyone but the family dog. And sometimes, unbelievably, the seers *did* bring back Rover or Rex—who no longer barked, but spoke actual English sentences. Also, in a really first-rate act, microphones could be hidden—just like they were all over 278 when Harry lived there.

It was the preying on the bereaved that Houdini despised—and with good reason. Not only were dupes paying hard-won money for tricks that were cheats (which the fake clairvoyants insisted were genuine), but their vulnerability often led them to muddy thinking and worse—to despair and abysmal sadness that was so complete they sometimes killed themselves. New York newspapers reported that

Doyle's May 1922 Carnegie Hall lectures resulted in suicides and murders. Among them, a desperate woman named Maude Fancher killed her baby and then drank Lysol, succumbing to the poison after seven days of excruciating pain. She left letters behind saying she wanted to be buried with her boy in her arms and—before she downed the fatal dose of lye—she wrote a heartrending note to Sir Arthur to tell him the tenets of Spiritualism inspired her to hasten herself and her child into the afterlife.

"IT'S JUST criminal what these vultures do to the unsuspecting," Houdini said. "Grief-stricken people at their lowest ebb...."

We were in his dressing room at 278. Houdini was packing for a trip to Washington D.C., pacing, tossing things Bess or I handed him from the tall chestnut dresser's drawers into a leather suitcase and talking to a *New York Mirror* reporter about testifying at the upcoming Congressional hearing—and even more importantly—trying to draft a bill that would make psychic pretense illegal. "Numerology, palmistry, speaking to the dead—all of it—right from the same junk basket," Harry said.

"What do you think would make intelligent, prominent men like Oliver Lodge or Arthur Conan Doyle believe in Spiritualism, then?"

Houdini caught my eye—fleetingly—but honest as he was, I knew he wasn't going to come completely clean with the reporter.

"Someone told me it's because secretly they fear death," Houdini said. "My God, thanks to Doyle, they envision paradise as 'Summerland' where you can play cricket, smoke cigars, and drink wine—like some species of eternal country club." He shook his head. "Really, do you think the God who created the majesty of the oceans and the mountains would communicate by tipping a table or ringing a bell? Or bother with producing a vile, phony concoction—like ectoplasm—from a medium's orifices?"

It was a standard argument, and Houdini spoke well and knowledgeably. But, just as I'd thought, he never mentioned the sex games or the deeper secret we'd caught onto investigating Evelyn.

"NO, LEONA," he thundered, thinking aloud and pacing in my tiny hotel room that hot July in Boston. "It's sex—and she uses it to wind them up like toys—but there's more. There has to be more. I know she's cheating—I caught her at it, for Christ's sake." He turned to me. "She had the unmitigated gall to tell me not to expose her because she'd just hate for her son to read in the papers that she's a fraud. Know what I told her? 'Then don't be a fraud,'" he said. His voice rose again: "I don't care who's tutoring her in magic—and mentalist routines—Thurston, Keating, whoever. No. There's something *else* going on in that house—and we have to find out what it is."

IT WASN'T as hard as it sounds, times being what they were. The well-to-do had many more servants than is common today, and turnover—especially among the nouveau riche—was high. I didn't take a job with the Trilbys, though; Harry and I were sneakier than that. He helped with the costume, listened to me practice my accent, sent me out to canvass the neighborhood, and presto! I was Mary Sullivan with a laundress's job, working in the enormous townhouse on Myrtle Street next door to Evelyn's lair. Back fence gossip was my entrée, and it didn't take more than a few days to share a smoke and make friends with my counterpart—a nineteen-year-old girl named Bridgett O'Meara—while we stood sheet to sheet (so to speak) pegging bed linen on our respective clotheslines.

"I heard yer mistress has witchy ways," I said as we stood—each on her side of a tall board fence—cadging a cigarette and shielded from sight by a towering old maple between the properties. "'Least that's the talk up and down the street."

"Who says? That Kitty Ryan, I'm betting," she tssked. "Sure, the girl couldn't keep from flapping her big jaws if the Holy Mother herself descended from heaven and told her to keep still."

"Sure, 'twas Kitty," I fibbed, "but I want to know is it true?"

Bridgett leaned further over the fence and dropped her voice. "There's plenty that would be afraid to work for the Trilbys," she said. "But about her bein' a witch or the place full of haunts—it's all eyewash."

"Jesus, are you sure?" I looked straight into her eyes and saw the truth.

"I'm not supposed to tell, I'm not supposed to even *know*, but I heard herself laughin', talkin' about the ghost in the machine."

"What does that mean?" I leaned closer into the boards until our faces were scant inches apart over the divide.

"Look here," she said stopping to peer around the yard and gaze up toward the tall windows. "This isn't the place to talk. When's your night off?"

"Tomorrow—just after seven," I said.

"Mine, too." She grinned.

"You meet me here as soon as it's dark, and I'll show you."

"I'VE GOT IT, Harry," I told him over the phone; he was at the Copley Plaza. I'd taken a powder—just walked off the laundress job that morning. "I know exactly what's going on during Evelyn's séances." I sat on the edge of the bed in my hotel room, hoisted up my gimpy leg to give it a rest.

"You were right," I said. "It wasn't hard at all. I made friends right away with the girl who washes and irons for the Trilbys. On Monday, I gave her half a seedcake I swiped from the kitchen; on Tuesday, I gave her two cigarettes. On Wednesday, she showed me the secret."

"That's very interesting, but I'd have to check my schedule, and Mr. Munn and I were just about to go to lunch."

"Christ, all right. I'll wait for you here."

"I have another engagement after that. So, yes, five o'clock would be about right."

IT GAVE ME several hours, and I thought I'd skip lunch myself and instead head to the library. Bridget O'Meara had talked about medicine and experiments, and though Harry was a voracious reader and researcher, I wasn't so used to it. Still, there was no harm in trying—especially in a university town like Boston, which also had top-flight hospitals.

I started with the wrong academic specialization, though—thrown off course by the fact that Trilby was a surgeon. My mind was reeling from reading card catalogs, checking references, paging through obscure and famous journals. Sun slanting through the tall windows at the medical library told me the time was getting short and I still didn't have answers. The desk clerk had been no help at all—he practically sneered at me; it was obvious he thought women had no business in medical libraries, especially those as important as Harvard's Francis A. Countway—one of the largest in the world.

"Damn it." Another dead end. I shut the heavy, blue-bound volume.

Across and down the long, blond wood table from me, a young man I'd scarcely noticed whispered, "What is it you're looking for?"

"Sorry," I said quietly. "I didn't mean to slam the book."

"You didn't ... but you look like you need some help." He got up and moved directly across from me.

"I don't know precisely."

He shrugged. "Be imprecise. I love a mystery."

"Well," I took a deep breath. "Something to do with fumes—and their effects on people—on what they perceive," I finished helplessly.

"What are you, a reporter? And why does Houdini care about fumes and their effects on people?"

Now I was startled.

He pointed. "You're using one of his programs as a bookmark." He smiled.

"Oh." I grinned back at him, relieved. "No, I'm not a reporter." I hesitated, unsure of how much to reveal. He looked earnest, sincere ... but what if he wasn't? He might be a reporter himself or a spy one of Harry's rivals had set on my trail to gain information about him. Trilby, we'd discovered, had a whole network of agents trailing Harry in Boston and elsewhere. I looked at him again. He was in his late twenties, a clean-cut, scholarly type. I decided to trust him, not knowing, of course, I was mirroring behavior Houdini would later indulge in—behavior at the time that would lead directly to his death.

HE WAS a medical student (whose name I never learned, unlike the name of the student—J. Gordon Whitehead—who would kill Harry in 1926 and be known the world over) and his special interest was in psychology and mental aberration. "One of my professors gave a lecture about this last year. I know exactly what you're looking for," he said. "It was written up in 1921 in *The American Journal of Ophthalmology* by a doctor named William Wilmer, and you can read the article yourself." He disappeared around the corner of a tall bookcase, and then laid out a heavy red tome in front of me, opened about halfway. He pointed. "Here," he said. "It's all about the fact that carbon monoxide has been shown to cause hallucinations and make people think they've had paranormal experiences—everything from pounding footsteps to ghostly apparitions to physical contact with entities."

"My God, how hard would this be to arrange..."

"Simple." He shrugged. "You just need a conduit—a vent or a fireplace or what have you—to pipe in the gas that comes out of the source."

"The ghost in the machine," I said. Bridgett O'Meara had taken me to the dank, cobwebby basement of the Trilby house and showed me the furnace and the switches and the pipes. And now I had just seen verifiable medical proof that Evelyn and Doctor Freddie were creating spirit activity using poisonous gas in small doses—which, sex games aside, made it even easier to fool educated, urbane men like the *Scientific American* committee and Sir Arthur Conan Doyle.

HOUDINI whistled. "You saw it, you read the article?"

"Yes."

"They see people? Hear voices? Feel like someone has touched them, you say?"

"It's all in the medical journal. Back in 1912, a whole family and their servants—they talked about feeling watched, hearing footsteps, seeing apparitions, and everything else that smacks of a classic haunting."

"You know, Leona, it's even more ironic—since Doyle was an eye doctor himself—when he was in practice." He grinned and said, "The *American Journal of Ophthalmology*." Then, unable to help himself, Houdini sat in the flowered chair in my hotel room, threw his head back, and laughed as loud and hard as I ever heard him.

HARRY never publicly revealed that Evelyn and Trilby were piping poisonous gas—in small, regulated amounts—directly into the séance room. I supposed it was because he'd already proven the medium was manufacturing routines as slick as any magician's. And though carbon monoxide is odorless, clearly they hadn't fouled the air when Houdini sat in on the séances—so perhaps they counted on the dark and Evelyn's sex lures to reel him in. But they underestimated his passion for truth—and his persistent wish that people *could* actually cross over and then communicate, so that he might have even *one* word from his beloved mother.

He spoke to Evelyn about it privately, though, he told me.

"You're playing a dangerous game, Edythe," he said, using her given name. "The effects can be cumulative—you don't want to harm yourself, do you?"

Evelyn tossed her reddish-blond hair. "I'm sure I have no idea what you mean, Mr. Houdini. I'm not worried about my health—after all, my husband is a doctor."

The Spiritualists might have considered his voiced concerns as prophetic. Twenty years later, during a séance, an aging, overweight Evelyn declared the entities had taught her—not just to levitate—but to fly, and she hurled herself from the rooftop of the Myrtle Street house, smashing against the pavement and landing in a crumpled heap of bone and blood five stories below.

Among the circle of sitters that night just after World War II, two men swore at the inquest she'd given no indication of her intent and that it happened so swiftly, no one in the group could have stopped her. Evelyn was, by that time, an ether addict, and I wondered if she still ramped up her occult reputation by using the carbon monoxide to flummox gullible clients. The two witnesses, it turned out, were, not surprisingly, Emory and Ford. Or, if you prefer, Fletcher and Fell. Dr. Trilby had died the month before; perhaps she meant to join him.

THE SIDEWALK placard screamed mystification from its wooden slant boards:

FLETCHER AND FELL
PERFORMING THE GREATEST TRIAD OF
MAGICAL AND SUPERNORMAL FEATS
SINCE THE LEGENDARY HOUDINI:
TWO NIGHTS ONLY!

There was a lot more ballyhoo and fanfare about show times, plus a carnie-era barker shouting come-on in front of the sign and accompanied by a scantily-clad assistant who shoved midnight blue flyers printed in white ink at every passerby.

I hadn't wanted to cruise the area around the Blue Moon Café in the Mary disguise again. So, on this late, chill Wednesday afternoon, just one day before my secret birthday and three days before the show, I'd dressed—as I had years before to help Harry investigate—as a stolid, no-nonsense nurse. Even with a coat covering the uniform, I knew people would be paying attention to the starched cap, the white stockings and sensible Oxford-tie shoes. I pushed past the wood and glass door then sat, hoping to find out more about Emory and Ford, the upcoming show, and why he'd tried to lure me in by dangling out the box jumper role when he was already in league with the medium. He'd called me crazy the last time we met and, except for those near-hallucinatory dreams I'd had in 278 over the past few weeks, I hadn't seen him.

A round Blue Moon paper coaster suddenly appeared atop the shiny, mahogany bar alongside my right elbow. "What'll it be?"

"A Pink Lady, please. Light on the gin."

The nearly bald bartender, who looked old enough to be Sam's father, nodded. "You got it." He began to whip the egg white into froth. "Don't get much call for these," he said, adding Grenadine to a shaker. "Not since *Esquire* put it on their list for the all-time 'Ten Worst Cocktails.'" There was just a hint of the Old South in his gravelly voice.

I shrugged. "I like them—they're sweet and a girl's girly drink. Jayne Mansfield's favorite, too, I heard."

"She doesn't come in here," he laughed, pouring out. Then, with a tiny flourish, he added two thin lime spirals and a cherry for garnish. "Pink Ladies—they were named for the Broadway play back before the Great War," he said.

I smiled. "Really? I had no idea."

I was just lifting the glass when he said, "Before you sip on that, I was wondering if you ever tried a Pink Shimmy. They were all the rage in New Orleans about twenty years ago—it's the same drink, only with a little cream. I could make one, if you want to try it." He glanced at Sam, who clearly had the other three or four patrons covered, and resumed his attention to me.

"Sure," I said, setting the glass back on the coaster. *New Orleans.* Home, at one time, to Emory—the medium who claimed he could conjure the dead.

"Did you live there?" I handed him a five, clasping his hand with both of mine and tapping smartly with my right index finger.

He grinned. "In the Quarter. Fifteen years." *Yeah-hs.*

"You have a slight trace of the accent," I said, looking directly into his eyes. I'd use cadence next, with certain inflections and rapidly uttered word substitutions to enter his subconscious. The funny thing was that consciously the mind registered the correct word— subliminally, the response was completely different.

"Most people think it's Brooklyn," he said.

"Most people *don't remember* what they hear, they don't have a very good *Emory* for that sort of thing," I rapped the bar once to move him deeper into the hypnotic state. "But you'll discover, that is you'll *mind*, I'm easy to talk to, and you can *fell* me whatever you like. *Fell* me anything at all about him...."

I WAS back in 278. Seemed to be sitting snugly against the edge of the séance table with two older gentlemen, both of them swathed in the red-jeweled pagri—*or turban—of a Swami.*

"You passed out, Leona, so we brought you here," said the jowly man on the right. He had heavy features, a thick chin. Something familiar about him, I thought.

"No, I was at the Blue Moon—"

"Too many Pink Ladies..."

"You." I pointed. "You put something in my drink!"

He nodded. I recalled his offer to make the Pink Shimmy—and wouldn't

Harry have loved the irony of that charming name. He'd been inwardly smirking, but I'd been so focused on my own agenda, it'd been easy for him to slip the Mickey Finn—probably chloral hydrate—into my drink. Misdirection. Christ, it works every time.

"Nobody likes a scene, Leona," the other man spoke up. "You were needed here."

I recognized the voice. Emory, I thought. What the hell is Emory doing back here at 278 with the bartender?

"More than a bartender, but perhaps you've forgotten. After all, it's been at least thirty years...."

Buried under the coarse flesh, the thick scalp that once showcased gleaming raven's wing hair with razor sharp parting, was a face I barely knew—and simultaneously knew too well: Arthur Ford. Not from New Orleans, but born and raised in Florida—southern accent and all. "Good Christ, Emory and Ford."

"You mean Fletcher and Fell." He grinned.

"CONTROL!" Fletcher shouted. And I felt both of them suddenly—fiercely—clutch my hands and wrists; their skin seemed reptilian, rasped like scales against mine. I was dazed from the drug, and my mind felt unsteady. "Control!" was something Evelyn's dead brother, Benjamin, had often called for during séances. I remembered, Harry'd told me, it had the dual benefit of creating a momentary distraction and convincing those who weren't already onto the medium's games that, because she was held tightly, Evelyn was clearly not the source of any phony paranormal manifestations.

"Control!" Fell echoed.

There was a cacophony of hideous overlapping sounds: the screeching of terrified birds; harsh, jangling percussion—like the clashing of tin cans flattened out and bits of metal strung together; shattering window glass; the sharp white crunch of breaking bones; and woven through the infernal noise, the voices of Fletcher and Fell cycled endlessly. The bookcases seemed to lean in and tower over us, and I felt a cold draft—the passageway, a throat beckoning, stood ajar.

Ah, God, I'd forgotten the lessons my history with Harry had taught me—spies and counterspies. For every undercover agent Harry privately paid, the mediums had employed a dozen, and I'd played right into their trap.

HARRY had railed against the plague of clairvoyants infesting Europe and America. Publicly, he focused on the way low-level wage earners and gullible indigents were robbed. But he also knew the séance fad and spiritualist folderol had been caught up by thrill seekers among the wealthy, and worse—in the highest government posts abroad, in Canada, among Senators and Congressmen here, even in President Coolidge's White House. "I kept it on the q.t., Leona," he often told me in a voice tinged with sorrow and something like regret.

I understood how he felt because I'd done the same. Harry had scads of operatives; famed among them was Rose Mackenberg—she was the one who discovered the government connections and who, for between two and five dollars, had been "ordained" a Spiritualist minister more times than she could count. She furnished Houdini with so many counterfeit charters for her own "church," he pasted them together in a huge roll and unfurled it with élan—like red carpet laid down before dignitaries—during his third act. Aware of Evelyn's own large network of spies (funded by the doctor and not a few wealthy industrialists and patrons), Harry decided Rose was too valuable to too many investigations to potentially compromise, so in 1926, he sent me to scope out Evelyn's act—her latest psychic manifestations—and though I was sure he'd give me a fair hearing when I reported, and of course I knew about the carbon monoxide, I was so convinced what I saw was real, I'd been afraid to tell him.

And, like him, I kept my silence.

BESS DYED my hair ice-blond, bobbed it, and dressed me like a millionaire's daughter. Now I was wearing the starched-white, nylon uniform, but I remember how the green silk dress she bought for me at Bergdorf's felt against my skin and the delicious, wintry touch of a fur collar on a "new silhouette" coat alongside my cheek. I reveled in the sway of the long opera strand of real pearls she let me borrow. Still, more ominously, I recall too vividly seeing Evelyn, seated at the trance table on Myrtle Street, her hazel eyes fixed on mine....

MY OUTWARD transformation, quicker than the time it took to establish two months of friendly correspondence with Arthur Conan Doyle under the name Miss Madeline Kendall—said to be a distant relation of the DuPonts—was ratified by my residence in an apartment Houdini set me up in at the luxurious Drake Hotel on Park Avenue and 56th Street.

"Doyle," Harry said while we sat in front of a sterling tea tray in the parlor at the Drake, a fire crackling to ward off the January chill, "raised something like $125,000 on his lecture tour and donated all of it to the Spiritualist cause." He picked up a pair of tongs and added a lump of sugar to the blue and gold Royal Doulton cup. "He answered Trilby when *he* wrote—and they became bosom pals—and you're going to gush on and on in writing. Use the hotel stationery and tell him something along the lines that the greatness—the incalculable depth—of *The New Revelation* and *The Vital Message* influenced you to become a believer," he said. "More importantly, offer to make a substantial 'anonymous' donation—and ask him to direct the funds to the proper channels." He paused, grinning. "Five thousand ought to cover it."

"Five—" I stopped. For five thousand dollars, you could buy a whole house. I knew Harry had a standing offer of ten thousand to any medium anywhere who proved genuine, but—

"Relax, Leona," he said. "Doyle will tell the Trilbys and get you in on a séance with Evelyn. And for five thousand," he said, laughing, just before he bit into a buttery crumpet, "you better watch out that phony doesn't shove *your* hands up *her* dress."

BECAUSE my foot lagged when I walked, I couldn't work on stage—too many of Harry's illusions depended on physical dexterity and being able to move quickly from one place to another during the exchanges—like *The Metamorphosis*. But I'd been well-trained by him during sting operations on phony mediums, so I wasn't overly worried about sitting in and faking my interest in the beyond at one of Evelyn's séances. I was sure I could carry it off.

In early March 1926, I dressed to the nines, armed myself with a transatlantic introduction from Arthur Conan Doyle, and, after phoning ahead to request a meeting for late afternoon, rang the doorbell at 7 Myrtle Street.

MIRRORING was my first thought. So much of life is mirroring. I'd been shown into the front parlor, and there was a tea table between us, sterling pot steaming—just like when Harry explained the gambit to me in my apartment at the Drake back in New York. Only now, Edythe Trilby *née* Walker, all wide-eyed and elegant-limbed, sat across from me.

I'd just withdrawn the cable from my beaded handbag, and her tall husband was entering through the wooden pocket doors, when she pushed a telegram toward me.

```
MADELINE D. KENDALL ARRIVING BOSTON
MARCH 4TH. STOP. VERY ANXIOUS TO MEET
EVELYN. STOP. SHE IS ONE OF US. STOP.
DEVOTED TO CAUSE AND VERY GENEROUS.
STOP. EXPLANATORY LETTER TO FOLLOW.
STOP.
                              ALL LOVE,
                              DOYLE
```

Edythe laughed. "My dear, Sir Arthur has preceded you, as you can see." She waved away the pink Western Union he'd sent me. "And besides, his letter arrived in this morning's post. He told us all about you—and we're thrilled you're in town. Is it your first trip?"

"Yes."

"Where are you stopping?"

"The Hotel Puritan," I said.

"Nonsense," Edythe said. "That's more than two miles away. We've plenty of room. Why not stay here?"

Too many of the *Scientific American* committee members had fallen into her honeyed trap, but I wasn't about to. "It's very kind of you to offer, but unfortunately I'm leaving town the day after tomorrow."

Edythe was quiet. She's not used to being refused, I thought. "Of course, next time I'm in Boston, perhaps I can stay longer, and meanwhile, we'll have time this evening before the séance—and tomorrow night, too, if you'll let me come again," I threw in for good measure.

She brightened at that. And then there were only the two tedious, nerve-wracking hours 'til we got through dinner served by a gloved butler and the others arrived and we all trooped up the stairs to the séance room.

HER CIRCULAR rosewood table—clearly not the same one used when Harry'd visited—was graven round with strange pale symbols—

JL_ЗЯОЯОЗ ᴛ˛Я˛2ЬМᴜᴾ

—carved into the dark wood that I barely had time to scan before the lights were dimmed. That first night, there were only five of us: Dr. Trilby—whose bald head shone with perspiration; a chirping older silver-haired woman named Mrs. Underhill; and a good-looking young man with a narrow, tidy mustache—like the one Douglas Fairbanks sported in *The Mark of Zorro*—introduced to me as Captain Mallory. Evelyn, dressed in a flowered kimono, sat between the two men. When she nodded, the same dove-gray-gloved butler who'd served dinner cranked up the "credenza" Victrola and a slow-paced version of the Varsovienne began to play softly; then he left the room.

There was a tall cheval mirror facing Evelyn's cabinet—the ordinary trifold standing screen she used to "gather psychic energies." *Standard equipment in the psychic biz,* Harry and I used to laugh—though the more adept among them used it similarly to the way Harry first used his own "ghost house"—with carefully concealed hiding spots built into it so he could retrieve whatever tools he needed to perform his escapes.

All our hands were knit; Trilby's—on my right—had the smooth, powdery feel of surgeon's talcum used inside the thin rubber gloves he wore in the operating room. The old woman's fingers—peeking from a pair of outsized lace evening mitts—were dry and brittle in my grasp. Mallory was wearing a gold pinky ring set with an onyx intaglio; it gleamed and flickered against Evelyn's long pale fingers in the low light of the wall sconce.

Odd, I thought: Whenever I accidentally shifted my gaze from the tabletop to the mirror, or glimpsed the sitters' reflection out of the corner of my eye, there seemed to be a great deal many more hands interleaving among ours—opening and closing, undulating.

Evelyn's eyes were cast down, but I couldn't shake the feeling she was slyly exchanging looks with Trilby and Mallory.

A pinpoint of light seemed to emerge from the mirror. *Penlight,* I thought. *Goddammit, where is that coming from? Maybe it's under her hair—a little surgical tape, and when she moves her head, presto! The beam—*

The record began to hiss....

When I looked away from the phonograph and toward the old woman, the mirror—which had been completely upright—tilted. *The butler did it,* I smirked inwardly, *with wires.*

On the Victrola, the scratching seemed louder—more grating—but I was aware of a tiny crepitating noise that clicked and skirled—like an eddy of autumn leaves caught in a gust of wind tapping against asphalt or window glass. It was a lonely sound, forlorn and desolate as the dying year.

Evelyn moaned once, softly, then began a low chant: *"Meroros, Arbmu, Arbmu, Meroros...."*

In the scant seconds before the lights went out completely and we were locked in darkness, the etiolated moving hands I could only see in reflection drew back from our living circle and each began to point— like spectral fingerposts. One by one, each letter briefly luminesced, then faded. In the mirror, the symbols were no longer reversed. I read the words, *Umbra Sororem* ... Latin?

Then, all at once, the room was bitterly cold and I felt a strange energy—peculiar and unsettling—like the sudden silence among birds and beasts just before an onrushing storm. But, in all my years, I'd never experienced any human equivalent to that dreadful sentience. I felt tension rising in the room, a very real sense of foreboding that seemed to charge the atmosphere. I was in the kind of blind panic that numbs the mind when the car you're driving is out of control and about to plunge over a cliff. There wasn't time to form coherent thought. *What's going—?*

In the icy blackness, my pulse skittered convulsively; my mind raced madly. *What is this? Not the carbon monoxide....* I could hear the old woman twisting in her seat and felt her ankle press harder against mine. She seemed agitated, and that didn't jibe with my understanding of the effects of the toxic gas.

In the heavy air, the mounting pressure—the electric sense something was about to explode—my heart drummed, my thoughts veered and lurched.

Get hold of yourself, Leona!
Calm ... be calm.

All right. This is just some new creepy effect Evelyn's showing off to her crew of believers, and any second now she's going to go into her ventriloquist routine—much easier to pull off without any lights—and start spouting in a fountain of Benjamin-speak.

Trilby and the young captain took up the chant; their voices rose and fell, merging with Evelyn's. Then, at the same instant—as if some deadly radio signal had flown in on a secret wavelength—all three of them began to whisper.

Then Evelyn picked up the pace. Faster and faster, until the words were no longer distinguishable. All three of them whispering so rapidly the sound was like the meshing blades of some huge machine, and it was a hundred times more ominous than if they'd spoken out loud.

"Meroros, Arbmu, Arbmu, Meroros...."

EVELYN raised her glance upward. Her eyes flashed neon yellowish-green, and I had the unsettling impression that her whickering mantra actually circled just above us—as if it were whirling headlong around and around a hidden track; the chant sucked all the energy from the room.

Then it began to generate its own hideous power.

Time seemed to simultaneously speed up, slow down, and stop altogether.

No, I told myself, *that's impossible*. I wasn't woozy and I didn't have a headache, so it couldn't be carbon monoxide. Could it be some other noxious gas? Or something—without taste or odor—served up at dinner that was just taking effect on me now? No, the butler had gone round—course after course—holding china platters with trout almandine, sliced roast of pork, artichokes, baked Alaska—and we'd each wielded the heavy sets of serving forks and spoons and helped ourselves. Trilby was a doctor—but I didn't see how he could've drugged the food and be certain the tainted portions would end up on his guests' plates. Evelyn certainly wasn't hazy. I'd have to ask Harry afterward, but I didn't think there were chemicals that induced hallucinations *and* clarity at the same time; I knew she was almost as dexterous as a professional magician, and there was no way to get hopped up and still make clever use of her hands.

It wasn't loud or penetrating, but my ears began to ache from the flickery noise of their chant; the pain intensified—the whispering honed itself until it sounded like steel knives being rapidly sharpened blade to blade.

Suddenly, I thought I saw a thin mist forming in the dark just behind Evelyn, and I strained to see it more clearly. There was a scattering of tiny lights, dim at first then softly sparkling as the skein of fog curved and began to loop round and round over our heads. I glanced at the mirror but saw nothing for several moments—until out of the corner of my eye, I saw a small shadow shape begin to emerge from the cheval glass. Above me, the whirling dust faded; the gleaming motes looked tarnished. Then, quicker than I would ever have believed possible, the shadow—now much more visible—grew darker than the dark itself; then it slowly spread like a canopy some three to four feet above the table. I smelled rotting meat, felt a terrible dead cold pierce through me like a shard of ice, and I gasped.

Oh Christ, what is this? What has she done?

The shadow shot filthy black tendrils that swept the very air aside, sinking downward like corpses hurled into the sea—and, stunned, with my mouth gaping, I felt the stinging vine-shape hurtling down my throat and anchoring deep inside me.

POSSESSION

I was supposed to return to Trilby's house on Myrtle Street the next night, but overcome by anxiety and illness, I couldn't. I'd spent the day retching, my knees growing colder against the black and white bathroom tile at The Puritan hotel while I hung over the toilet and disgorged dark, brackish water—again and again.

I was no socialite, and I never called Evelyn with polite regrets. Instead, my phone rang at least five times from early afternoon on. Three of those times, warily lurching toward the bedside table, I picked up. Twice, there was nothing but silence followed by a sharp click. I was too ill to even curse the callers' childishness and, overcome by another wave of nausea, reeled back to the bathroom. A half hour later, I was feeling a little better, sturdy enough to gather the Dixie cup of shaved ice—my mother's old remedy for queasiness—that was already nearly melted. Then I'd try lying propped against the pillows on the bed.

I sipped, savored the feel of the icy chips in my mouth and against my tongue.

The phone trilled.

I was too tired to care. I left the candlestick portion on the night table and merely picked up the bell-shaped receiver. *Maybe it's Harry,* I thought.

"Hello ... Hello?"

At first there was only the void of silence, and I was about to hang up when—just as if whatever entity on the other end of the line knew it had hooked me by pretending it was already gone (or had been cut off in the modern electronic wasteland)—it began to screech.

There was a welter of sounds so hideous I cringed. Then I blanched with terror and actually felt the blood draining from my face: The cup, I saw, was now bubbling and a small pale cloud of steam rose above the paper rim. *Boiling? No, room service sent up a bowl of chipped ice—* it was still sitting on a tray the bellhop had set on the low dressing table twelve feet away. In slow motion, I reached toward the nightstand for the cup; it suddenly catapulted, flipping over and scalding the tips of my fingers. My heart jolted with fear. A geyser whooshed with the sound of bursting pipes, shot up from the ladies' vanity—instantly fogging the mirror behind it, flooding the bowl, hotel tray, and tabletop, then cascading over the edge onto the tufted bench.

My hand stung, but I was aware of a growing chill in the air, of the fine hairs on my arms rising. Jungle yawps mingled with the sound of flames and screams and insectile buzzing. Foul demonic noise. A Bosch painting come to life. From what seemed like a hundred voices, language—whether words or phrases or cursing—I had never heard and could not identify punctured that ugly caterwauling drifting in and out. It was very old, *ancient*, I thought, and then a more terrible idea crept inside me: I don't think—whatever it was they were speaking—had ever been uttered by anyone human at *any* time in this world.

With that grotesque notion, my head spun, I fell onto the bed and into a darkness I wish I could call sleep.

I WISH I'd consciously known back during that early spring of 1926 Harry only had six months to live. Maybe I would have focused less on the inner turmoil—the ugly, lingering aftereffects of the session with Evelyn that plagued me; less self-absorbed, I might have been stronger and not so vulnerable. I was teetering just before his final tour. Then, when he died, the self the world and I called "Leona Derwatt" was gone for many, many years.

November, I've since learned, is the time of year most conducive to demonic activity. By the 12th of that month, Houdini was already buried underground and I was in the hell of a mental ward called Highgate, located behind old stone walls about twenty-three miles north of the city and straddling the Connecticut border—the first of what would be a series of confinements.

AFTER the Congressional hearings in May, when the Spiritualists threatened Houdini and were up in arms, and the bill to make psychic readings illegal failed to pass, Harry decided to take the summer off before what would turn out be his last tour in autumn. He spent much of the time working on his book about superstition. You may or may not know, he also hired H.P. Lovecraft to do some research and fiction writing. I was functioning—admittedly at a low level—as his secretary. I was supposed to answer the phone, type up his notes and the manuscript, but the July heat, rising relentlessly through the house to the office in the attic, sapped me. It was August now, but back on July 22nd the temperature in Central Park was the highest ever recorded— 104 degrees—and the first of what would turn out to be six major hurricanes ripped through the Southern states.

"You're awfully pale, Leona," he said, suddenly peering over the top of the pages clutched in his hand and looking at me.

He was too kind, too loyal to dismiss me, but Houdini was dictating that morning while I sat, pen poised, taking down his words in shorthand because he'd discovered earlier that month that, left to my own devices, I tended to fall into an odd dream state. Mid-word, mid-sentence, my fingers would hover completely still—like disconnected starfish—just above the keys while, for a minute or an hour, I made no progress. I merely stared at the whitewash of the plaster wall in front of me. I had no awareness that I'd stopped and couldn't recall (even to myself) what I'd been thinking. I *wasn't* thinking; my mind was completely blank. Now it had happened—not while copying pages or listening to the rhythmic drone of recorded speech—but while he talked and paced in front of me.

"You're dripping—are you all right?" I was startled back into semi-focus, saw his eyes track a bead of sweat that coursed down my chin and landed on the back of my right hand.

"Oh!" I cried out. It was unnerving, embarrassing—I'd watched him follow the drop of perspiration without any consciousness on my part that it *would* fall—something even a three-year-old child would have known.

"You're not well," Houdini said.

I shook my head.

"Let's take a break," he said. He glanced at his watch. "10:30— hmm ... well, it's not quite time for an early lunch, but maybe some iced tea or a snack is in order—something, anyhow. Why don't you lie down? Or better yet, I'll ask Julia to bring us lemonade and we'll both go sit in the backyard for a half hour or so."

"COOLER HERE," he said after he dragged a couple of wrought-iron chairs and a tiny table for two under a huge, old elm behind the house. He swigged lemonade, and I was acutely aware of the ice clinking in his glass.

I tapped a cigarette nervously against the gold case.

Houdini took the case from my hand, opening it and peering at the inscription. Then he gave a small grin, trying to lighten the mood. "I'll have to have your case engraved again if you don't rest up and really get well," he said.

Get well? What did he mean? "My secret birthday," I mumbled, then stopped.

"Yes, you remember, I gave this to you—well, Bess and I gave it to you—the first day you were able to walk—after," he paused. "After that terrible bout of polio."

His eyes wouldn't meet mine; he was looking down at his hands. "That was a special day, all right," he went on, opening and closing the case so it seemed to catch the brilliant sunlight. "The physical therapist was so excited she was practically choking. 'Mr. Houdini,'" he said, his voice going high, "'come quickly! Hurry! Miss Leona is up and she's on the crutches, walking!'"

He gave it to me for my secret birthday. I don't understand. "I—" I put my right hand up, then—fingers pressed to hair and flesh—began digging into my temple.

Harry suddenly took hold of my arm. "Leona, what's wrong?"

"It's the sun," I began. "My God, the sunlight arrowing off that case is nearly blinding me." I felt my eyes well with tears that made prisms of the gold light—flashing now in a thousand colors, ten thousand idiot shapes.

THE HEAT and the approaching storms—that's what I remember about the summer of 1926. It was so hot, horses collapsed in the streets of New York; babies and old people in tenements grew pale, gave up, and died without a whimper. Fans whirred. Tar melted. Icemen cursed when their deliveries from the blockhouses upstate failed. Over all, there was a hush—as if that infernal heat took everything—even sound—from humans.

The hurricanes, when they came, brought no relief. Their time was marked by the chaos of raging winds and rain so heavy trees were uprooted, houses were ripped from their foundations and floated—bobbing, ugly flotsam—down streets suddenly turned into wild rivers.

The world, I thought later, had been preparing for the great loss, for Houdini's death.

IT WAS September, and Harry was packing again for what was to be a five-month tour. The suitcases and trunks were open, half-filled with shirts and collars and suits. I was shuttling back and forth between his dressing room and the attic office to retrieve papers and books he wanted to bring along on the trip, rapidly filling a medium-sized wooden packing case. I was kneeling on the rug, adding some notes he'd taken about the occult and Masons for a planned article and squaring them alongside a bulky folder that contained his written plans for a College of Magic he envisioned would rival Columbia University, when I felt his hand on my shoulder.

"More?" I teased. "You'll need another trunk—or three—Harry."

He held a worn manila envelope, its string neatly wound around the faded red paper buttons. "They're photos," he said, opening the folder. "I was going to put them in my trunk without showing them to you, but...." He shrugged. "I changed my mind and I want you to see them." He began to slide the pictures out. "One of my operatives collected these—on the sly—from a closet hidden in the Trilbys' cellar." It was a thick stack. Harry turned away, motioned me to follow, and began spreading them out neatly on his bed. But there were too many and they began to overlap and cover one another.

"They're children," he said. "All children."

"All boys..."

"More than a hundred," Harry said.

Something in his voice caught at me. "Who are they?"

"We don't know all of their names. We couldn't trace a lot of them."

The photos, I saw, were not copies. They were the originals, and many of them had a creased look, as if they'd been handled a lot. I ran my fingers lightly over the image of a small boy in a badly made Fauntleroy suit standing in front of a potted palm on a studio carpet, a worn lop-eared bunny clutched in the crook of one chubby arm. He couldn't have been more than three years old. The photograph paper had a subtle blistered look here and there; that's when I understood this—and the other grubby pictures like it—had been cried over by mothers. Mothers who missed their sons.

"This is all that's left of these children," Houdini said. "They've disappeared."

"What did Evelyn and Frederick do with them?"

"Not even my paid secret service can find out, Leona," he said, shaking his head. "We don't know if they're dead or lost in orphanages or poorhouses." He glanced down at another boy (who could have been Houdini himself, back when he was Ehrie Weiss in Appleton, Wisconsin) perhaps nine, posed with his arm around a younger sibling, both of them barefoot by a swollen creek, a string of fish lying on the grassy bank, then moved it aside. He swept his hands over the spill of photos across the bed. "I can't forget these children. Their faces haunt me. I look for them every time I visit a sick ward or a school. They haunt me, Leona," he finished. "You keep the photos, okay? I don't need them—I see them every time I close my eyes."

MANY PEOPLE know Houdini died on October 31ˢᵗ—Halloween— 1926. What they may or may not know is that it's surmised that his appendix was ruptured by a sequence of unexpected blows to his lower abdomen.

He'd fractured his ankle earlier that month while being hoisted for the Water Torture Cell. Then, in Montreal, while resting on the sofa in his dressing room, he was visited by several art students from nearby McGill University. Indefatigable even with a broken bone, Harry had lectured there vociferously three days earlier on the subject of

Spiritualistic frauds—in particular Evelyn and Lady Doyle. And, as usual, he made the headlines. *Houdini Blasts So-Called Psychics, Singles Out Lady Doyle and Boston Medium Evelyn.* Word got around quickly and Sir Arthur was miffed.

On Friday the 22nd, Sam Smiley, one of the college boys, was making a sketch of the magician at Houdini's request.

There was a knock on the door and J. Gordon Whitehead, who was returning a book Houdini had lent him, entered and sat down. They talked of detective fiction, but Houdini evaded the young man's questions about the nature of the miracles in the Bible. Spiritualists, he knew, often claimed Jesus had been a medium who performed miracles. Then, Whitehead turned—according to the others—the conversation to Houdini's supposed ability to withstand even the hardest blows to his midsection. But Harry, weary and in pain, spoke about the iron strength of his biceps. "Go ahead and feel them!" he invited, flexing his forearm. But the young man—by all accounts over six feet tall and close to two hundred pounds—bent over and suddenly began to pummel Houdini, who was still half-reclined on the couch.

The artist and his pal protested, shouting "Are you crazy?" Whitehead got in another three or four jabs before Houdini finally collected himself enough to say, "That will do."

Over the next few days, Houdini complained repeatedly about severe abdominal pain, but he wouldn't see a doctor and performed at each of his scheduled shows.

No one, it transpired, named J. Gordon Whitehead attended McGill University.

WHAT IS even less well-known is that, just before Houdini left Montreal two days later, he was sitting reading a newspaper in the lobby of his hotel, The Prince of Wales, when three or four roughnecks approached him. One of them, a big beefy type, suddenly punched right through the paper directly into Houdini's abdomen. "You shouldn't have done that," he said, rising; then he walked slowly through the exit.

IN DETROIT, the next stop on the tour, a physician diagnosed appendicitis, but the magician refused to cancel the sold-out show. Houdini went on. After the first act, his temperature was 104 degrees. He mustered his will and again went back out on stage. He railed against phony spiritualists and mediums and somehow finished. Then, as the curtain fell after the third act, he collapsed.

DURING the emergency surgery, it was noted that his appendix, now gangrenous, had ruptured. Newspapers reported "pus overflowed from Houdini's abdomen and spilled onto the floor of the operating room."

By the 29th, peritonitis had set in and his condition was even more critical. A second surgery was performed; afterward he was certainly weak, but on Saturday he was awake, aware. He wrote a letter to a friend and scribbled a note I'd find years later:

Mirror = Speculum Magic. Also called 'The Devil's Looking Glass.' John Dee (1527-1609): Horace Walpole (The Castle of Ontario) owned it from 1771. I'm not sure why this suddenly seems important but it is. Strange pictures in my head. What are the Myrtle Street gang doing with mirrors? Ask L — she knows....

The deadly sepsis continued to seep into his bloodstream.

On Sunday afternoon, the 31st, he told those at his bedside, "I guess I can't fight this anymore." His eyes fluttered, then closed.

He was gone.

THE SPIRITUALIST mediums had cause to rejoice. Their arch nemesis—who had deprived them of untold dollars by exposing their wiles and tricks—was dead. Lady Doyle's control, Pheneas, had been predicting since 1924 that Houdini was doomed. Benjamin, according to Trilby's records, had said more than seventy times during the preceding year, "Tell Houdini I will see him soon." Naturally, this news had been spread far and wide among those who believed. Trilby even received letters from Evelyn's ardent admirers wanting to know if

Benjamin had reached out to influence the Canadian student—thereby causing Houdini's death. And now that there was no one to further expose Evelyn's fakery, she began a very successful yearlong tour to promote Spiritualism and her psychic abilities.

THOUSANDS attended Houdini's funeral at the Elks Club on November 4th. His fellow Masons from the St. Cecile Lodge scattered boughs of evergreen—symbols of immortality. One of the members of the Society of American Magicians carried a ceremonial magic wand—signifying power—broke it, then laid the halves atop the casket.

Thousands more lined the streets outside, milling, weeping, obstructing traffic until at last the way was cleared for the hearse and a procession of more than fifty black cars—headlights shining—winding slowly toward Machpelah cemetery, where he'd be laid to rest alongside his beloved mother.

IN HIS WILL, Harry had asked that all of Bess's letters to him be placed in a black velvet bag to be used as the pillow for his head in the coffin. Julia and I assembled the letters to give to the undertaker, but before we sewed up the seams, I slipped in three tokens of my own.

First, I put in a plain little gold-plated ring. It wasn't worth much—or anything, really—but my father, who kept Houdini as a hero—had given it to me on the day of my Holy Confirmation.

Second, I added the program from the first night we performed together at the Hippodrome back in 1919—along with a faded yellow rose he'd given me that evening just before the show.

And finally, I took up a sheet of heavy ecru stationery bordered in black, scented it with rosemary oil for remembrance, and added a brief note of my own:

October 31st, 1926
To Harry Houdini--who brought magic
to my life, love to my heart,
and depth to my soul--from your Leona
Dream of me softly, gently ... always.

HARRY left me $30,000—which may not seem very like much now, but when you consider the average income in 1926 was a scant thousand dollars a year, it was a lot. Invested for me by one of his friends, it has ensured that, during my confinements, I can afford to go to private hospitals. Not that they're a whole lot better than the lunatic asylums run by the state. Still, I have my favorites—Grasslands, Highgate, and Silver Hill among them—where longtime staff know me and dispense with a lot of the drearier admission rituals used to subdue anyone (read everyone—U.S. psychiatry is democratic, if nothing else) with a proclivity toward violence.

Over the years, on the whole, I've been a model patient. Only one time did the goons in white clamp down on me, straitjackets in hand, syringes at the ready. And it wasn't my fault—really, it wasn't.

I was at Grasslands—no, Highgate—when it happened.

For a few days, the voices had been tormenting me again. Not the sort of voices the schizos hear—although it probably won't surprise you to learn it's impossible to explain to a psychiatrist (or an alienist, as they were called back in '26, when I was first hospitalized after Houdini's death) that these voices aren't the same at all.

"I'M NOT hallucinating, Dr. Barnes, honestly I'm not."

"Leona...." he said, his voice a hint, while casually tapping the capped end of his fountain pen against the shining, dark walnut surface of his desk. Waiting for my answer. "Well?" He leaned back, spun away in his chair—to give me some extra mental space. When I talked, I knew he'd be listening for any lies. Instead of his avid round face and piercing eyes behind the rimless glasses, now I merely saw the tip of his nose and part of the bald dome at the top of his head. "Well?" he repeated. When I didn't reply, he quoted from a report one of his night spies obviously made; the voices are always worse—louder—at night. "*Meroros Arbmu.*" He spun back and gave me a sharp look.

I glanced down. "A chant," I began feebly.

"You were not *chanting*, Leona," he said. "You were answering someone. And you may have confused or fooled others—"

"Others—that's exactly the point—"

"Other personnel, other professionals—*even other doctors*—whether here or at some other hospital," he said, bearing down, "but not me." He shook his head. "You're a smart woman, and I guess you thought you were being very clever—and I admit for a while you had me stumped. But 'always go back to the basics'—that's what I learned from my mentor—or your 'favorite Viennese headshrinker,' as you call him—and that's what I did." He pressed a button inside the right-hand drawer of his desk; a tape whirred briefly. Then I heard a hoarse voice begin to whisper "*umbra sororem....*"

"You'd be surprised how many patients claiming to hear voices respond in English, French, German, Dutch—and yes, even *Latin*," he said. "And *all* of it spoken backwards." He pointed at the recorder. "Shall I reverse the tape this time and play it the way the machine *actually* picked it up?" He pressed again. "*Meroros Arbmu ...*" it hissed. He began, absently, to tap the pen again. He knew it annoyed me.

"I don't speak Latin," I said.

"No doubt at some point you memorized a phrase or two. And that might've been plenty—as I already said—to confuse some doctors. But it's not going to get you off the hook around here—"

"It isn't my voice," I cut in.

He'd stopped the irritating tic—now he was taking notes. The pen-scratch sounded like the metallic hiss of a dagger snicking through paper. "All whispering sounds pretty much the same." He shrugged. "And it's beside the point. Whenever you're deteriorating, starting to go downhill, it always starts with the voices," he said, then paused, staring hard at me. Years later, I'd learn that day he'd written down *inappropriate affect.* "What are you smiling at?"

"I was thinking it was very much like Houdini of you to have recorded my room secretly."

THAT NIGHT, it began to rain inside my room. The voices were very loud.

I knew better when the staff accused *me* of stopping up the tiny sink in the corner by the window than to say: "It wasn't me, I didn't do it." By then the walls—even my bedclothes—were dry. Only the white hospital towel that had been rolled inside a yellow slicker I'd never seen before—and that had been wedged against the door to keep the water from spilling out into the hallway—was still sodden.

While a plumber tore at the short u-shaped pipe, a nurse with a pen and a clipboard stood ankle deep in water and asked me what happened.

I knew better, but it still took every ounce of self-control I had not to answer by repeating out loud what the voice, urging suicide, had whispered, shouted, and finally screamed at me all night long: "Do you know you can drown in just a teacup of water?"

I GOT a reprieve because the plumber vouched that the pipes were ancient and corroded, and because Barnes believed me when I said I was not angry and, more importantly, that I didn't want to hurt myself—or anyone else.

It was rescinded less than twenty hours later, when the falling rocks shattering my meager furnishings and gouging holes in the wooden floor materialized.

IT STARTED as a shower of pebbles that awakened me. Before I could even get out of bed, it escalated to what felt like a dump truck of gravel pouring onto me, its dust choking me. I was dazed, stunned, still sitting in the dark, blinking to get the grit out from under my eyelids, when glossy black rocks made of obsidian began to clatter loudly down, and then pound the room.

BY THE TIME I was shrieking with pain, my desk and dresser were already splintered. Lamps were knocked over, the porcelain sink was smashed. Curtains were torn, the bed had collapsed, and I was bleeding.

No matter how much money you had, private hospitals, with their emphasis on making patients well, weren't equipped for—and didn't want to deal with—wanton mania. As far as the staff and Dr. Barnes were concerned, I'd injured myself in the process of violently destroying my room.

The rocks, needless to say, were gone.

And, needless to say, I spent quite a long time in an asylum run by the state.

IN THE candlelit library at 278, I blinked slowly. Adjusting to light, sound, scent. I knew, mentally, I hadn't been there for a while, but I was uncertain about the blank spot—not just its duration, but what had happened, might have happened ... and what activity, what thoughts had filled that—to me—ominous gap? Memories? Some kind of trance state? Induced by whom exactly, and how?

I immediately recognized that woozy-swimming-up-from-the-sea-bottom sensation that arises after fainting or coming to when time has been lost (completely different from waking out of sleep or even anesthesia), and I felt a nasty spurt of panic. If you've read Thigpen and Cleckley's bestseller, The Three Faces of Eve, *you'll understand the overwhelming dread I felt. Dr. Barnes—along with the rest of my numerous shrinks—has assured me again and again I'm not a multiple personality. I'm not.*

All right then. Inhale; long, slow exhale.

The last thing I could remember was that brief reminiscence about the green silk dress from Bergdorf's, about the way Bess had transformed me from head to toe, from waif to sophisticate—

Now I was alone. But, yes, that's right ... I'd been sitting between Emory and Ford—their hands clamping down so hard I thought my bones were being crushed.

Just before the room had gone completely dark, before the darkness that was the beginning of unaccounted-for time (minutes? hours? surely not a whole day) the candle flames had flickered back and forth so rapidly—like a film run at impossibly high speed—their yellow gleam was transformed into an optical illusion: They seemed to flatten out to the horizontal.

I winced at the sudden pain in my fingers, looked down at Emory's knitted into my mine, and in that weird flamelight, caught the wink of a gold pinky ring set with an onyx intaglio.... Where had I seen it before?

Associate, Leona, I admonished inwardly. Goddamit, think!

But I kept seeing flashes of hazel eyes that went neon yellowish-green, of dove-gray gloves, of lace mittens and bare hands, tall mirrors, glittering smoke, black shadows ... and ... and there were voices ... whispering. The hideous chant that cut through me, rasping like blade sharpened against blade.

The circular rosewood table my hands now rested on was cut with peculiar graven symbols. Runes, perhaps? Or were they letters?

I stood up, raising the candelabrum to see if I could puzzle out their strange shapes, when the moving light revealed the open passage. An old black-and-white photograph was lying on the threshold—as if it had accidentally fallen from some secret cache inside the turned bookcase.

Seconds later, I held it between my hands.

Timeworn ... creased ... blistered paper.... It was a picture of a boy I didn't recognize. Huge brown eyes—silked by the astonishingly long eyelashes so common in children—stared at me. He was three or four years old, wearing a cheap velvet Fauntleroy suit and cuddling a well-hugged woolen rabbit in one arm. Lazy clouds drifted high in the studio backdrop. His tiny shoes were spit-shined bright against the carpet.

I ran my fingers over the photograph where it had gotten wet....

I was aware of the creaking my starched white uniform cuffs made rubbing over the paper. Then there was a fluttering sound—like wingbeats from a thousand birds—and I turned.

Photos—like cards flying from a magician's deck—poured out of thin air and rattled onto the tabletop.

In five long steps, I was at the séance table and my gaze was riveted on the dull rosewood that was now almost completely covered.

Photos—hundreds of them—and all of them, children.

THE SOUND *of weeping began to ricochet around the library. Piercing sobs echoed against the walls, growing louder and louder until they filled the room, spiraled up through the house into the attic, out the roof and, I thought, surely must have reverberated in the heavens. Broken mournful tune. Mothers who'd shed tears over the loss for half a century, died in pain lamenting bits of memories: a snaggle-toothed smile, a pair of dark brown Sunday-best shoes, the smell of soft blond hair after it was washed with drugstore shampoo on Saturday nights.*

The lost and disappeared children imprisoned in those old sepia portraits wept, too. Wept at being torn from shabby homes and mother-arms, from all they'd ever known. Wept into the thin pillows of cold orphanage beds, and the still colder soil that filled their graves.

The din of that ceaseless wailing tore at me, and my cries mingled with theirs until, I supposed, none of us had tears left, and there was only the night's thick silence.

"HARRY! My God!"

He stood in a blaze of light that seemed to come from everywhere and nowhere all at once. His face was younger, his hair dark and thick, no longer grizzled with the wisps of gray that I remembered, that he'd once told me wistfully had begun to salt his hair when he was still in his thirties. When he'd told me the same bitterly cold night in Chicago, I recalled, that he loved me, but I was so very young and he was nearly twenty-five years my senior.

HE HELD his hand out and I stretched mine toward him and, between us, there was a small blue flash, a tiny crackling. A magician's flourish. He smiled, brushed the skin of my knuckles with a soft kiss. Then he straightened up, his eyes met mine. He cupped my hand in both of his as if between his warm palms he held some long-coveted treasure he wanted to touch just once, delicately—a butterfly unique in all the world, or perhaps the secret light that glimmers on angels' wings.

He drew my hand—still in his—toward his chest, then laid it against his heart.

AND THEN this was the way it was, how it was to be a woman at last and to feel Harry's long body covering my small one, to see his face transfigured with wild joy, to peer over his broad shoulders into the blazing light that haloed him completely, spilled in a luminescent cascade from his aura—his soul—and washed over mine.

AFTERWARD, we lay naked in each other's arms and he told me many things—all without uttering a single word aloud. He'd filled my body, and now he filled my mind with an urgent montage of images.

Look, Leona ... do you see that? And that? We should have told each other so much more back then—with everything explained, nothing omitted or held back.

My cheek nestled against the damp curling hairs on his chest, and I felt him kiss the crown of my head.

Oh, Lee, there's so much I want—no, I need—you to understand about the past, and the future ... and our time is very short.

HE WAS telling me a story—not with the sequenced logic of beginning, middle, end—but through the loops and swirls, the joinings and counterpoints of association that mysteriously cohere. I imagine, if what they say is true, the swarm of words and pictures, sound and meaning, of brief epiphany and abbreviated memory Harry showed me, was like the instant panorama of your life flashing before your eyes when death is near. And, like that mind-altering immersion, you understood yourself completely for the first time. Understood the nature of every interaction with every human you'd ever known. You became that person. You grasped their true thoughts and feelings, the motives and intent—and disregard—behind every deed:

DID IT begin with the children? Spirits are attracted to houses with children....

MAYBE at first it was a game between Edythe and Frederick Trilby. Marriage stales, boredom sets in, and there are only so many illicit five o'clock cocktails and swank charity balls and fancy-dress hospital fundraisers to flirt in new gowns, to hold forth in tuxedos. The same old faces crowding you. After a while, you can't tell one event from another—or one face for that matter.

City rain leaves sooty marks on the windows, and the rain is better than the grimy, end-of-a-Boston-winter snow, and the new maid hasn't a clue how to bank a fire properly, and the new bottle of gin you got from Roscoe tastes like kerosene, but he says there won't be any whiskey coming down from Canada until next week, and one February evening, deep in cognac and deeper in the gloom of lengthening shadows, a magazine containing an article about summoning spirits is cast aside on the sofa and Edythe discovers she has a natural flair for parlor tricks.

Entertain themselves and friends....

Frederick likes to be first at anything: "My dear, you're really good at it and it's all the rage and we've never lagged behind the social scene. Now we'll be in the forefront. No one knows you're cheating—"

A shared secret gives a little fillip, an anticipatory vibration of thrills to come—especially as her skills grow and the ruse becomes more elaborate.

Snickering in front of the bathroom mirror, watching herself practice speaking in her dead brother Benjamin's gruff voice, and Frederick, standing behind her, nuzzles her neck, cups her breast and says for the first time in their marriage, "I'm so proud of you."

For a long while, no one—except the two of them—realizes that sometimes during the séances in the room at the top of the house it's not Edythe pretending to be Evelyn pretending to be Benjamin: it's something else. Edythe thinks (as crazy as it might be) even though her mediumship started as a prank, that Benjamin's spirit has *actually* come through. It has to be Benjamin, because they were very close as brother and sister, and this spirit knows all about her—knows things she's never told anyone else; the kid stuff they shared—like the time back in South River they sneaked into the Star Theatre on Ferry Street to watch a Keystone comedy, used the "admission" money to buy hot dogs. She must've gotten a bad one, because by the second reel, she threw up in the balcony.

She'd missed Benjamin and thought about him often; within a month of when he first appeared at a séance, she realized she could talk to him all the time—day or night, anywhere in the house. She got in the habit of pouring herself a snifter or two of brandy before bedtime and, while Trilby snored upstairs on the second floor, she sat by the fire in the front parlor waiting for the cheery, smart aleck signature whistle that always preceded one of his visits—even in the séance room.

Soon he was not just recalling their shared past or commenting on the present; he began to drop hints about her future. "Listen, kid, Trilby likes to keep his hand in during the séances," he snorted laughter because her husband always controlled her right hand. "Just loves all the publicity, and wow! Now he's a regular pal of Sir Arthur's—but unless you do some fancy footwork, people are going to start to wonder what exactly happened to all those little English boys, not to mention the other kids he yanked out of Podunkville, Ohio—or wherever."

"What can I do?"

"And you like all the attention, too. So, the ones that aren't too damaged—if you know what I mean," he said, grinning, "you put them on a train and send 'em to some poorhouse or orphanage—but nowhere too close to home."

He kept telling her to get rid of the kids—disappear them. But she didn't do it—she got caught up in the day-to-day thrill of the séances, the correspondence with her fans as her fame spread, newspaper articles: *"Evelyn" Newest Back-Bay Psychic Sensation!*

Then one night, her crystal brandy snifter sailed up from the cocktail table, gathered speed, and flew across the room, shattering when it landed inside the fireplace. "Have I got your attention yet?" he screamed at her. A gout of yellow flame leapt out following the trail of droplets and, the next thing she knew, the stack of newspapers they kept in a tidy wooden box on the hearth was blazing. "You do what I tell you," he shouted.

She put the fire out pretty quickly—but not before it singed two treasured Persian silk floor pillows she'd bought in a *soukh* in Morocco. After that, she paid attention when Benjamin told her to do something.

Sometimes, to her wonderment, only she could hear him. "Go ahead," he told her during a dark séance, "open your kimono and spread your legs. George is dying for a feel, and all you have to do is use your free hand to nudge his between your thighs. He's good looking, all right. I know you want him. And guess what, sweetheart? He wants you! You can't tell me you haven't noticed the way he looks at you. He doesn't even bother to pretend he's not staring at your gorgeous tits. Mmmm ... getting wet just thinking about it, aren't we?" He laughed. "He likes to think of you all wet and slick, sitting on his face—but that's for later. For now, finger fucking in the dark will do. Well? What are you waiting for? Ha-ha—I know what you're thinking before you do—don't tell me you're worried about Trilby? Are you kidding, he'll get off on it! It's not like he can do anything with his prick, except hose piss out of it. Look," he sighed, "all right—for now I'll make sure the rest of these dopes don't tumble to what's up—you never mind *how* I can do it. *I can.* Go ahead. Yeah ... yes, that's right. He's wondering how you'll taste if he puts his tongue in your cunt. Georgie-boy tastes pretty good himself ... why don't you find out how good he tastes?"

SIR ARTHUR was convinced her powers were genuine. He also maintained that occasionally mediums had to cheat when their psychic reserves were low, help out the spirits to manifest effects. Benjamin, he asserted, was proof of her abilities. Still, she practiced—even secretly hiring a medium-mentalist-magician named Emory to teach her the rudiments. Benjamin had told her it would be a good idea—together, they'd create the most vivid séances ever recorded. Benjamin was right. It wasn't long before the *Scientific American* was interested—and even more interested when she came on to one committee member. He'd told her that would happen in one of her dreams. He came to her in dreams a lot. And once again, he was a hundred percent correct when he told her that, one day, Houdini himself would be sitting to her left at the séance table.

But, it always bothered her that, when Houdini came to 7 Myrtle Street that hot July, Benjamin refused to help her, was nowhere to be found.

No wonder he called her a fraud. How could she possibly hope—

with her third-rate conjuring or that clumsy business ringing the bell with her foot—to hoodwink the world's paramount magician?

WHY DIDN'T she know it couldn't be Benjamin? Houdini, clearly tuned into my thoughts, squeezed me, then brushed away a sheaf of hair that had fallen over my eyes. Deception, I heard him say inside my mind, is a demon's stock-in-trade. With just enough truth mixed in to confuse a human's reason, Leona....

EVEN THOUGH Evelyn loved being a psychic, loved the excitement Benjamin created—whether it was bringing her another sexual conquest or levitating furniture or predicting what would happen, she wearied of the feeling of oppression that gripped her. She could put on a mask and appear cheerful and witty when Benjamin was around and showing off for the sitters, but she was depressed when she was alone.

She decided she'd make Robert Willis, one of the committee members—who was wealthy and had movie-star good looks—marry her. What had been done once could be done again, and she'd grown up lower-middle class—and that was putting the kindest construction on her family's circumstances—but she'd snagged Dr. Trilby. The Boston Brahmin had fallen for her—hard.

She begged Benjamin to help her trap Willis, but all he'd said one evening while she undressed was "Lose the phony pregnancy-pillow."

"But it was your idea, Benjy—"

"No, it was *your* idea," he insisted. "And, besides—it's not working. This chappie ain't gonna go fallin' for that old chestnut, sister. Throw it out."

Instead, she bought spell books in a witch's shop in Salem, and Robbie found her alluring and adored her, but she couldn't wrest him from his marriage. Finally, he broke it off. It was after the tearing argument they had one rainy March afternoon and he stormed out of her house—not caring that he slammed the back door so violently he'd bent the hinges—that she began to drink more heavily. She spent a lot of time sitting at her dressing table, feeling sad—and worse, certain her looks were beginning to fade. When she went out to shop, friends she ran into remarked she appeared very tired. Perhaps, they said, the psychic manifestations—all the energy and focus she needed to create the effects—was draining her? In the mirror, she saw a woman who wasn't even thirty but looked fifty.

SHE'D TAKEN the car to Salem on a whim. The weather changed and it began to sleet, so instead of driving back to Boston, she decided to take a hotel room. Inside The Black Crow Hexery, she lingered over the herbs and candles and crystals, opened several books to check the precise spell ingredients she needed. The shopkeeper, Edythe noticed, was eyeing her—but not because she seemed to be anxious about stealing. Her face had been splashed around in plenty of newspapers; maybe the woman recognized her.

"Looking for something in particular?" she asked.

"I'm not sure I can describe it precisely," Edythe said.

"Try me."

SEVERAL hours later, Edythe straightened the sheets on her bed in the Hawthorne. She scrubbed her mouth where her lipstick had smeared and put on a blue cashmere robe. The owner of the hex shop had been more than helpful; she'd hung a closed sign on the door and, carrying the heavy book she said Edythe needed across the street to the hotel, shared the witchery of her secrets *and* her body. Women, Edythe had found over the time since Benjamin returned to her in spirit, could provide the occasional pleasant diversion from men. They made you just as hungry after sex, she thought, grinning. She ordered steak with trimmings, a bottle of red wine, and a cognac for afterwards. Then she sat to wait and opened the Book of Shadows.

"YOU CAN send the spirit into someone else and still retain control," the shop witch had told her. She stroked Edythe's midriff. "It works, because you create a shadow—of yourself. If it's someone who doesn't know what you're up to, a mirror is the easiest way to touch them covertly. Then, your auras will mingle...."

MY GOD! I thought. Mirrors ... touch! That's why at the séance that night on Myrtle Street, the old woman was wearing lace mittens and Trilby's hand was coated with talcum powder; the butler even kept those gray gloves on when he cranked up the Victrola. But there was more—Evelyn had a definite intent. The chant—shadow sister—was an invocation. She got Mallory—Emory!—to help her! She realized it was some kind of malevolent spirit they managed to conjure up, and she sent it inside me. That bone-gripping cold, those foul, coiling threads....

"But why me?" I said, searching his gray-blue eyes. I felt soiled, ashamed.

Whispering into the deep recesses of my mind: Somehow—maybe through that thing that called itself Benjamin—they discovered I was the one who got Evelyn discredited in the Harvard study by using one of my spies, and it nearly capsized her mediumship.

I felt his hands in my hair, fingers playing gently. He went on: I was also the one who persuaded a member of parliament to look into what Trilby had done with the boys from England who'd gone missing. Trilby wrote to Doyle that the government wouldn't take just anyone's complaint seriously—not unless it came from a well-connected Brit. And they tried to figure out who it might be. They thought it might be Maskelyne—the famous British magician—but neither of them realized the M.P. was Harry Day. A business associate, but also a good friend to me for more than twenty years.

"I don't understand," I said.

Evelyn figured if an entity attached itself to you—because you and I were so close—she could use it to manipulate you. But her goal, ultimately, was to hurt me—one way or another. She didn't reckon on the fact that her mirror ritual would let in a whole hoard of the blasted things.

"What do you mean, Harry?"

The lower entities—the ones who whisper or shatter glassware or, say, levitate furniture—their job is get your attention, begin to break down your will. Once that happens, usually people are afraid. If they're not fearful, these shadow spirits—who were never human to begin with—find any weakness and exploit it: anger, addiction, depression ... a sense of isolation. It doesn't matter what. They feed off negativity. Any of it—all of it—paves the way for more controlling demons.

"So did Benjamin leave her?"

He shrugged. Any of those foul things could pretend to be Benjamin then come back when Evelyn's self-doubts about her skills began to creep in. Even at séances, people get bored after a while with the same routines—if you're not going to constantly find new sitters you've got to vamp up the phenomena. Not to mention, Evelyn liked being famous, and if you're going to keep reporters hungry, you need newer—and bigger—manifestations.

"Just like showbiz," I said, giving his chest a quick kiss. His hand traveled lower, and I felt him softly stroking the length of my back.

She liked being famous. She worried about losing the spotlight. She wanted him back—probably invited or called him—or even thought about missing him. Once these things attach to humans, they're always just around the corner, lurking in the shadows, waiting to pounce on a person's vulnerabilities. So, he shows up again, and at first, it's like old times—reminiscing about their childhood, laughing at Trilby behind his back ... and he even rewards her—now she's not just ringing a bell or raising the table a few inches, she can produce flocks of screeching blackbirds, levitate in and out of the fifth-floor windows. But soon she's getting deeper into the booze and rummaging through Trilby's medical bag for sedatives and opiates. The really sick, malicious trap it laid was to hook her into the kinky games, then take away her looks so no one wanted her, but she still craved—needed—sex. It wasn't just the liquor or the drugs that aged her so quickly—it was because something inhuman rode her back.

Bess drank a lot, I thought. I wonder—

Harry nodded. They sent her a shadow picture. It came to 278 on Julia's day off, and Bess opened the mail. I don't know if she felt anything or if she just threw it in the trash, but it doesn't matter. Because once someone—even an innocent— touches the photograph, the entity's aura will mingle with theirs and cause whatever damage it can. Keep on causing it, too.

"So they did send those kids in Canada to kill you, and they knew you'd had subacute appendicitis in the past, and that those punches would probably cause a rupture."

Those things tell the future—another way to suck humans in, at least for a while. Anyway, Evelyn spread the word and her crew got the message that I would ignore the pain and keep performing. And that's what I did.

They're very destructive. That's all they seek, all they ever really know. He laid his hand softly against my cheek, tilted my chin up, and our gaze met briefly.

For that second, I thought, we weren't just looking in each other's eyes, but into each other's souls.

"Evelyn eventually killed herself," I said, *unable to tell this vibrant, loving man—who held me so warmly—how many times I'd heard voices urging me to commit suicide.* "And for years, I was in and out of asylums."

THERE WAS a series of sharp, cracking sounds across the room. I sat up abruptly, my gaze fixed on the table. All the photos were snapping forward—standing rigid, vertically on edge—and my breath caught in my throat. In an instant, still upright, they began to waver, rapidly rocking back and forth.

"Harry!" I was too stunned to do more than lift my hand to point.

Lightning flashed. Then, one by one, the children's portraits began to float higher and higher, gathering speed, spiraling up and circling counterclockwise—until the shape they formed looked like the funnel of a tornado and the cloudburst above it. Their small, wise faces—haunting eyes staring out at me—a spinning, airborne carousel. The temperature in the room suddenly plummeted, and the noise of those madly whirling pictures took on the fierce rush of wind in a storm. I pulled my knees up, lowered my face against them, huddled under my arms. In the onslaught, I heard the intense, jagged roar of thunder again and again until my eardrums ached and all sound seemed shut behind a wall of ice—and very far away.

WHEN I opened my eyes, the room had gone silent. The velvet window curtain had been pulled aside; in the moonlight, I saw a man—pale buttocks thrusting out—bent over in the act of drawing on a pair of tuxedo slacks. A wrinkled white dress shirt lay nearby on the floor amid a scattering of cuff links, imitation pearl studs, a clip-on bow tie, socks, and shiny black shoes. A jacket hung crookedly—as if slung there hastily—from the back of one of the chairs at the séance table.

"Harry?"

"Yeah—sure. Harry. Whatever you want." He'd retrieved the shirt and was putting it on over his naked chest. He turned to sit on the edge of the chair; I caught a glimpse of kohl, smudged under his lower lashes and streaked down one cheek as he was tugging on short black socks. Now he began shoving his feet into the tight patent leather, a finger inserted—behind one heel, then the other—for leverage, like a shoehorn. He used his palms to quickly smooth down his wiry hair. Why was he rushing to get dressed? There was a highball glass on the table, and a battered-looking flask stood among the drift of pictures.

"Harry," I said again—but I wasn't sure I'd spoken aloud. Thoughts and images raced through my mind. Harry always wore garters—I knew, because when he caught Evelyn faking, he'd even published a pamphlet explaining how, sitting next to her in the dark, he'd rolled up the cuffs of his trousers, and she couldn't slide her foot forward to ring the bell because her stocking caught on the buckle of his garter. And undergarments—he wouldn't put on a tuxedo with nothing on underneath it. A clip-on bow tie? Wrinkled clothes? And Houdini didn't drink. Period. A sudden flash: Emory's specialty—bringing back the makeshift dead for lonely widows and widowers, phony spirits of departed loved ones to be clasped in passion once again.

"Who are you?" I demanded. He had the jacket on; he was taking a plain, white envelope from one of the pockets. He opened it, peered in.

"Listen, sister—" He was thumbing the contents rapidly. I saw his lips move … counting. He was counting something—

Cash.

"You son of a bitch," I shrieked. "You goddamn dirty whore!" I lunged at him, hands hooked into claws. In one springing leap, I was on him, my nails shredding the flesh on his cheeks.

"Mr. Ford!" he yelled. "Mr. Emory!" His voice was wheezy with shock.

"They can't help you!" I shouted. Contempt fueled my rage. He'd profaned the memory—the sacred memory—of the world's greatest magician, the only man I'd ever loved. A man loved and respected and *honored* by millions. I spit at him. The instant his hand went to his face to wipe the gobbet, he blinked with disbelief—looking at his wet fingertips stippled with blood and saliva. It was all the opening I needed, and I dug in harder. "I'm going to gouge out your filthy eyes," I screamed.

IN THE MIDST of my fury, a muffled, frantic voice from somewhere on the first floor carried on the air and came through to me:

"Operator, operator! We need a doctor! She's gone absolutely crazy!" Pause. "No. We can't calm her down—we can't even hold her down! There's two of us, and it's like she's suddenly got the strength of a giant!" A second brief pause. "No, I don't know *who* her doctor is! Get someone from Bellevue! Immediately!" Final pause. "278 West 113th Street. And hurry … please *hurry!*"

I BLANKED out, but not completely. Instead, I drifted in a strange, brown haze—like dimming lights on the verge of losing power, blinking off for an instant, and then brightening again, but always at a lower wattage. I flickered in and out of an odd dream state where a peculiar *knowing* came to me that alternated with actual sounds around me: shuffling feet, bits of conversation, the meaty smell of blood, the swoosh-gargle-clatter of a mop first being plied across a dirty floor then thrust all the way to the bottom of a metal bucket:

"HURRY UP, wouldja? That stupid bimbo operator might call the cops—"

"You told her Bellevue, right?"

"You were standing right there. You heard me."

"I heard *you*; but I didn't hear *her*! You said—and I quote, 'She'll fuck him, I guarantee it. After that, it's good-bye, Leona, hello Houdini *and* Fletcher and Fell—'"

"She did fuck him. You heard it. Hell, we watched it on the cameras," interrupted the voice I recognized through my mental fog as Emory's. "Wouldja ever have believed that smart little Jew prick would've had so many wires running through this goddamn rattrap?"

The mop swished over the floor, and I smelled blood and shit.

"It was your idea to buy it. 'They're going to tear it down; we can pick it up for a song. And think of the publicity,' you said. *Magicians New Owners of the House Houdini Built.*"

"We did get press—and I still say we'll get more: *Magicians Discover Houdini's Secrets: Hidden Legacy in Harlem Brownstone*," Emory said.

"Yeah, but you said, 'Just give her half an hour of pillow talk time, and she'll start reminiscing about the good old days with him. We'll find out plenty.'"

"And we *would* have—if that idiot rummy didn't decide one fuck was plenty, because it was high time for a drink. I told you to be careful about those drunks that hang out all day in the Blue Moon," Emory said.

"Listen, he might've been in there every afternoon the last three weeks when I was behind the bar, but I never once saw him talking with nobody. But, I mean, *nobody*. He wanted the job—didn't ask no questions, didn't care. How was I supposed to know she was gonna go batshit?" Ford, I thought; of course—the other one has to be *Ford*. And, where's there's smoke, there's fire: Fletcher and Fell—the real *Fletcher and Fell*—with all the veneer and trappings of cultured voices and fake, smiling good manners stripped away.

"Batshit? She tore out his fucking eyes! Thank God for those cameras—but I still say it's lucky I got in here so fast and dropped him with the andiron before he started running all over the goddamn house—with blood everywhere—"

"Wait! Hold up on unrolling the carpet. Get that splotch over there by the door first—"

The sounds of knee joints cracking, the wet rasp of a sponge being used to scrub; Emory, stooping down to work on the drying gore. "Almost done, and we'll keep the lights real low when the lunatic-snappers get here."

"How long's it been since you called?"

"Maybe five, ten minutes—give or take. Even if they use the sirens, it'll take 'em a while to get here from downtown and across to the West side. Especially with the traffic this time of night—the shows over on Broadway are just letting out—"

"Well, you never know—it's still a good thing we tossed him in the cellar before you called."

"Yeah, and a *better* thing he was the one rented the tuxedo. Christ, the blood."

"Anyway, like I said, he was a loner. And it's not like they'll get very far trying to track him down at the Y. He did odd jobs to pay for his room, week to week. I checked. The rental place will just chalk it up as a loss. Meanwhile, it didn't cost us a cent. The money's right here. Even the down payment—minus what he shelled out for the tux—it was still in his pants pocket."

"Yeah, but just to be on the safe side, it won't hurt to cut the shop-labels out of the pants and the jacket before we bury him," Emory said. "We can line the trunk of your car with one of those canvas tarps in the basement. Soon as they leave."

"Where's this place again, that you want to ditch him?"

"Pelham Bay Park—in the Bronx—twenty-seven hundred acres, and plenty of swamp to accommodate our tuxedo-clad friend downstairs—"

"Give me a hand with this rug—it's a heavy bastard. Take that end and we'll turn it around."

Grunting noises. A curse when Ford drops his end.

"Hey, did she just move?"

I felt their eyes train on me and I lay limp, scarcely daring to breathe.

"No way. I gave her enough chloral hydrate in that hypo to stun an *ox* for three hours."

A thud-smack when the last of the carpet flops against the floor. Sounds of a cloth being whisked over the rune-graven tabletop, the children's photographs flicking against each other, being tidied into neat stacks.

"You rinsed off the andiron, then smudged it with blood from where she clawed you? Okay, good. And we're straight on the story? Old friend in the biz, she stopped by for cocktails. We were all drinking, then she passed out on the couch. We left her, went upstairs to watch TV. Coupla hours later, we hear her going nuts down here. You came down to check. She'd ripped off her clothes and, when you came in, she attacked. Like a tigress. You couldn't hold her, didn't want to deck her, but you were struggling with her, shouting for me. I took one look and ran for the hypo."

Gritty scraping sound of the library bookcase being pushed back into place, sealing off Houdini's secret passageway....

"Okay that's it. Done. Go ahead and turn down the lights, Arthur—they'll be here any minute."

VERY SOON, I knew, *yes, very soon* there'd be the abrupt squeal of brakes, the chunk-chunk-chunk of ambulance doors slamming, and hurrying footsteps racing up the stone stairs, the doorbell gonging....

ARTHUR ... Arthur—like chiming in my mind. Then the thought broke off. The ignominy of it—being found here naked on the floor. Christ, if I could wish myself disappeared—*Ar—thur* ... an echo, louder inside my head. Sudden memory upwelling: Arthur Conan Doyle and his conviction that in order to effect his escapes, Houdini actually *dematerialized*. The brief reminiscence now mixing with ... filtering *through* that awareness, that peculiar knowledge you're certain—soul-deep certain—is accurate. Truth. Realization that actors and artists and the very ill are more acutely sensitive to entities, that it's also easier to connect with spirits while asleep or dreaming—and surely the brown haze of sedation, the drifting half-in-half-out state conferred by the chloral hydrate has sent me to the same astral plane ... where I now watch the swift parade throughout the centuries, true occurrences: all variations of objects and people disappearing, transported across spans that range from feet, to yards, to miles. Sometimes thousands of miles. A wedding ring long buried in the coffin with a beloved husband appears on a grieving woman's matrimonial bed during the Italian Renaissance. A coveted silver tureen is stolen and hidden in her own house by a charwoman in nineteenth-century England; less than an hour later, having been promised an excellent price by the crooked pawnbroker in the next street, she eagerly hurries back to retrieve it— and finds in the short time she's been absent, it has disappeared; a fourth century Chinese poet absently takes up his bamboo writing brush—looks upward as phrases are already beginning to form in his mind—looks down to place the first black stroke and finds himself two miles away, sitting by the koi pool in his lover's garden. Teapots and grandfathers, golden retrievers and alchemists—countless items, untold numbers of men and women and children. Mysteries ... magic.

Now I suddenly recall hearing that, shortly before he died, Houdini told the young doctor who sat by his bedside he'd always wanted to go into medicine, and he regretted it. Shocked, the resident protested. "But you're the greatest magician of your age; you've made thousands of people all over the world happy. People everywhere admire and respect—even love you. I'm just an ordinary surgeon—"

Houdini cut him off. "Maybe that's true, but the difference between us is that you actually *do* things for people—but," he shrugged, "what I accomplish is only trickery. You're real. I'm a fake."

Outside, I heard the distant wail of a siren. "No, Harry," I mouthed silently, sudden tears upwelling. "The others were the fakes—Evelyn and Emory and Ford. You were no fake."

VOICES, the rush and scuffle of white-jacketed attendants—human keepers—carrying a white cloth prison for me, what would be, I knew, just the first of many.

"Harry," I whispered softly, "You told that young doctor the Spiritualists were going to have a field day when you died."

I paused. Someone rapped on the glass in the front door,

simultaneously thumbing the doorbell.

"You said you wouldn't lift a finger to delay—even for a single minute—the joy of meeting your beloved mother and seeing her in heaven. You also told him you'd been sincerely trying to help those Canadian students—the one paid for his sketches, the one you kindly lent the book to, and that no man should regret dying on account of a good act."

Footsteps in the entryway once graced long ago with potted ferns on marble pedestals and an ornate mirrored hall stand. "Where is she?" I hear someone in the foyer ask in a low voice. "In the library. This way."

"Harry, the children still cry out for you. I'm crying, too."

Sensing the press of shoulders in the hall, hard breathing. Hearing the metallic click of the key turning to unlock the door.

The curtain's ringing down, Harry.

I bite down on my lips to keep myself from screaming. They'll be on me in a moment....

The door snicks open, but the feeble light from the hall is eclipsed by dazzling, glorious wildfire to my left. I turn to see it, gasp.

Harry stands transfigured before me, in the classic pose of saints: arms welcoming, hands lightly held at the level of his slim waist, palms up.

My Harry in a blaze of Christ-light.

Did you not remember I would hear even the smallest—the least—of your pleas? That, if you believed in me, I would never forsake you? Even in your darkest hours, I have always been with you; I am with you always and shall be evermore.

Salvation in a slow, beatific smile.

I jump to my feet and run to him, not even bothering to look behind me, listen to the hectoring shouts.

Houdini's arms spread wide now, and as they rise up, I see that even his magician's cloak has metamorphosed from dead black silk to brilliant white.

I vault inside the circle of his arms; they lock around me, his cape enfolding my nakedness, my bleeding shame and sorrow.

I feel his heart pounding against mine.

And presto! I vanish.

EPILOGUE

<u>Physician's Notes for October 31st, 1956:</u>

Case #67120, Leona Derwatt, white female, age 56.

Patient continues to display violent outbursts, which have worsened in the last ten days to include verbal abuse of staff, damage to hospital property, and an ill-conceived attempt at suicide by tearing bedsheets and trying to swallow ripped portions in order to suffocate herself.

Telephone consultation and review of previous medical records while under the care of Dr. Jack Barnes (Highgate, private institution, Armonk, New York) indicate this is longstanding behavior, which <u>typically</u> escalates this time of year.

Diagnosis: Adult schizophrenia with attendant delusions, auditory and visual hallucinations. Severe depression, anhedonia. Anxiety and obsessive-compulsive disorders.

Recommendation: Continue close supervision.

Security: Restraints. Continue maintaining patient on locked wards ONLY.

Treatment: Continue Stelazine/antipsychotic and ECT/electro-shock therapy.

Signed,

Peter Thompson

Peter Thompson, M.D.
Staff Psychiatrist, Bellevue Hospital

ACKNOWLEDGMENTS

Thanks go to Culpeo S. Fox for her striking cover illustration, to Amy York for designing the cover, to Lori Ann Leonard for helping with some tricky formatting issues, and to Terri Gillespie for her excellent proofreading skills.

Weldon Burge, Editor
Smart Rhino Publications
August 2015

AUTHOR'S NOTES

Like my unreliable narrator, Leona Derwatt, (whose name, by the way contains a clue to her personality—and Patricia Highsmith fans have a heads up here), I fell madly in love with Harry Houdini at a very tender age. I think I was perhaps nine or ten when one golden Sunday afternoon the film with Tony Curtis and Janet Leigh was on TV, and that was enough for me. The very next day, I was at the library looking for a Houdini biography and was pleased when, upon bringing it home—and even before I read it—my father offered the information that Houdini's real name was Ehrich Weiss. He clearly knew a bit about the man, too.

As a grown up, researching this novella, I confess to not only reading many more biographies, but some fifty or more books including those written by Houdini and about him and on subjects ranging from history to automatons, from mentalism to spiritualism, from magic to illusions. I also watched every video I could find, including but not limited to Houdini's own movies, Doyle's *The Lost World*, and film subjects like the fairy photographs, magicians, illusionists, and much more. In short, I had myself a grand old time. Better still, at the end of all this reading and viewing, I was still madly in love with Harry Houdini.

Sir Arthur Conan Doyle proved slightly more problematic. I still remain a huge fan of the Sherlock Holmes canon, but I wasn't happy to learn that Doyle was quite so gullible when it came to the paranormal and some of the less-than-genuine mediums he championed. I guess the turning point for me (and I admit, Houdini influenced me) was Sir Arthur's insistence on Lady Doyle's lately acquired paranormal gifts. Houdini had big problems with the reading she did for him beginning with the fact that she drew a cross at the top of the page of automatic writing and he was Jewish! Another troublesome area was that Lady Doyle was ostensibly in contact with his beloved mother on the exact day of her birthday (no mention of the date came through during the reading) and, worse, she did not communicate in her native tongue. To put it bluntly, when she was living she spoke no English; and Houdini did not accept the Doyles' insistence that she learned it in the afterlife—and neither do I. This is not to say they weren't sincere in their beliefs, but the séance stretches credulity for even the most rapt believers in the other worldly and Houdini's disappointment (later in print) signaled the breach in their once mutual admiration and friendship.

All that said, there are some real life people I need to thank. First, Paul Leyden. I had an aha moment shortly after reading the excellent book *Hiding the Elephant* by Jim Steinmeyer shortly before watching (again) *The Illusionist* and *The Prestige*. It occurred to me that the first one was a love story topped up with magic, and the second film was a revenge story topped up with magic and that both of them were displaying some very standard 19th century illusions (brand-spanking-new and therefore amazing at the time) and that some story or movie idea could be wrought based on the magic of the period. It was Paul who gave my interior creator the big green light: Use Houdini: damn the torpedoes, full speed ahead. I love talking to him, anyway; it's always great, creative conversation and in this case, one better: genuine inspiration. So, thank you, Paul.

Huge thanks to my first readers: Janice Morgan (whose enthusiasm keeps me tippy-tap-typing and whose critiques are spot on) and Lisa Lane (also, in this case Lisa functioned as my editor extraordinaire). More input and assistance from these wonderful and trusted first readers:

Corrine De Winter (who provided a writer's retreat and—even above and beyond that incredible gift— listened to the damn thing besides); and also many thanks to Michael Hughes, Elizabeth Blue, Terrie Lee Relf, Marie Zbytek, and Robert Dunbar.

It goes without saying, enormous thanks go out to my agent, Cherry Weiner, and to the very talented and extremely intelligent Weldon Burge of Smart Rhino Publications—with whom I sincerely hope to publish many more stories and books.

Finally, I'd be remiss if I didn't mention there was a lot of very lively debate among all my editors and myself regarding the many stylistic oddities of the novella—so if there is any nose-wrinkling, please keep in mind that the impetus for breaking so many rules was at my behest and the onus is entirely on me.

Lisa Mannetti, Author
August 2015

ABOUT THE AUTHOR

Lisa Mannetti's debut novel, *The Gentling Box*, garnered a Bram Stoker Award, and she has since been nominated three times for the prestigious award in both the short and long fiction categories: Her story, "Everybody Wins," was made into a short film and her novella, "Dissolution," will soon be a feature-length film directed by Paul Leyden. Recent short stories include, "Resurgam" in *Zombies: More Recent Dead* edited by Paula Guran, and "Almost Everybody Wins," in *Insidious Assassins*. Her work, including *The Gentling Box* and "1925: A Fall River Halloween," has been translated into Italian.

She has also authored *The New Adventures of Tom Sawyer and Huck Finn*, two companion novellas in *Deathwatch*, a macabre gag book, *51 Fiendish Ways to Leave your Lover*, as well as non-fiction books, and numerous articles and short stories in newspapers, magazines, and anthologies. Recent and forthcoming works include additional short stories and a novel about the dial-painter tragedy in the post-WWI era, *Radium Girl*.

Lisa lives in New York in the 100-year-old house she originally grew up in with two wily (mostly) black twin cats named Harry and Theo Houdini.

Visit her author website: www.lisamannetti.com
Visit her virtual haunted house: www.thechanceryhouse.com

ALSO BY LISA MANNETTI:

THE NEW ADVENTURES OF TOM SAWYER
AND HUCK FINN

Tom and Huck have reincarnated as twin white cats, and they're now familiars for a modern-day witch—and, of course, they want to be boys again! This whimsical, often humorous novel has been masterfully written by Bram Stoker Award Winner Lisa Mannetti. Mark Twain would be proud! Published in Adult and YA editions. Available in Kindle and paperback.

UNCOMMON ASSASSINS

Hired killers. Vigilantes. Executioners. Paid killers or assassins working from a moral or political motivation. You'll find them all in this thrilling anthology. But these are not ordinary killers, not your run-of-the-mill hit men. The emphasis is on the "uncommon" here— unusual characters, unusual situations, and especially unusual means of killing. Here are 23 tales by some of the best suspense/thriller writers today. Available in Kindle and paperback

ZIPPERED FLESH 2
More Tales of Body Enhancements Gone Bad!

So, you loved the first **ZIPPERED FLESH** anthology? Well, here are yet more tales of body enhancements that have gone horribly wrong! Chilling tales by some of the best horror writers today, determined to keep you fearful all night (and maybe even a little skittish during the day). Available in Kindle and paperback.

SOMEONE WICKED
A Written Remains Anthology

Avaricious, cruel, depraved, envious, mean-spirited, vengeful—the wicked have been with us since the beginnings of humankind. You might recognize them and you might not. But make no mistake. When the wicked cross your path, your life will never be the same. The 21 stories in the Someone Wicked anthology were written by the members of the Written Remains Writers Guild and its friends, and was edited by JM Reinbold and Weldon Burge. Available in Kindle and paperback.

Made in the USA
Middletown, DE
02 October 2015